Cesare Cantù

Lord Byron and His Works

A biography and essay. Edited, with notes and appendix

Cesare Cantù

Lord Byron and His Works
A biography and essay. Edited, with notes and appendix

ISBN/EAN: 9783337011680

Printed in Europe, USA, Canada, Australia, Japan

Cover: Foto ©Raphael Reischuk / pixelio.de

More available books at **www.hansebooks.com**

LORD BYRON AND HIS WORKS:

A BIOGRAPHY AND ESSAY,

BY CESARE CANTÙ.

EDITED, WITH NOTES AND APPENDIX,

BY

A. KINLOCH,

LATE CAPT. 36TH REGIMENT.

. . . . "The biographer of Byron has yet to arise; the work of Moore, which is the best known . . . . cannot be regarded as final," &c., &c.— *Belgravia*, Feb., 1869. WM. STIGAND.

LONDON:

GEORGE REDWAY, 12, YORK STREET, COVENT GARDEN.

PRINTED FOR THE EDITOR BY THE
SHROPSHIRE GUARDIAN NEWSPAPER COMPANY, LIMITED.
OFFICES: 4 CLAREMONT STREET, SHREWSBURY.
1883.

BY PERMISSION,

TO

HIS EXCELLENCY

THE MOST HONOURABLE

THE MARQUIS OF LORNE, K.T.,

GOVERNOR-GENERAL OF CANADA,

THIS LITTLE WORK IS

RESPECTFULLY DEDICATED.

PREFACE.

Adverting to the most recent attempts in the present day to revive the interest in a life which the Memoirs by Moore might be supposed sufficiently to perpetuate, we may, in this brief epitome of Lord Byron's career and works, merely say, that neither Professor Elze, Castelar, Madame de Boissy, nor Mrs. Stowe seem to have entirely exhausted the subject.

To indite, however, much that is new regarding a Poet, who, if not the greatest of English Bards, is one who, from his chequered life and almost matchless rhyme, has interested this country and perhaps the world more than any writer—save, it may be, Homer or Shakespeare—has not now been attempted. The records of his life and the universality of his works may be found in the Folio Catalogue of the National Library in the British Museum, where 112 pages attest the facts above averred. In this little volume, some indulgent criticism of Lord Byron's poetry and some mild censure of his moral delinquencies have apparently been essayed by the Italian legislator and historian, Cantù, whose work, originally merely a printed lecture, has been amplified, through the kindness of subscribers, by the Editor of this volume. We may trust, therefore, that with all its imperfections, voids, or repetitions, the present little work may be found by the reader both useful and acceptable as a kind of compendium of the life and works of Lord Byron.

Cesare Cantù, the writer of the brilliant essay now given, was born, it seems, in the first decade of this century, at Brescia, in Northern Italy, though some biographers assign Cantù, near Milan, as his birthplace.*

He became Professor of *Belles Lettres*, at Sondrio;

* *Vide* Appendix.

afterwards, as a member of the Italian Parliament, he was one of the few belonging to the Ultramontane party, who, in spite of liberal and patriotic ideas, sided with Papal Rome in politics. As a literary man, he has greatly contributed to the education of his country, and is the author of some popular religious hymns, whilst as a writer of fiction he has even more celebrity.

His greatest work is the *Storia Universale*, a General History, 35 vols., published in Turin in 1837, though he has besides written much on Italy and its literature.

His last work appears to have been *Storia del Popolo e pel Popolo*, 1871.

A. K.

SUBSCRIBERS.

Most Hon. His Excellency The MARQUIS of RIPON, K.G., Viceroy of India.

Most Hon. His Excellency The MARQUIS of LORNE, K.T., Governor-General of Canada. (2 copies).

Rt. Hon. The EARL of NORTHBROOK, G.C.S.I.

Field Marshal LORD NAPIER, of Magdala, G.C.B. (2 copies).

General SIR WM. F. WILLIAMS, Bart., G.C.B. (2 copies).

General C. E. FORD, R.E.

General SIR ARTHUR PHAYRE, G.C.M.G., C.S.I.

Colonel The Hon. C. H. LINDSAY, C.B.

CHAS. W. KINLOCH, Esq., late B. C. S.

Mrs. HITCHINGS.

Mrs. KITSON.

Col. J. J. GRAHAM, R.M.L.I., C.B. (2 copies).

Capt. RICHARD BURTON, F.R.G.S., &c.

R. DURNFORD, Esq.

FRANCIS CAMPBELL, Esq., Foreign Office.

Right Hon. A. J. MUNDELLA, M.P.

Messrs. STEPHENSON, TUCKER, BASSETT, TABOR, COURTHOPE, JOYCE, RITCHIE, (2 copies), SANDFORD, POOLEY, R. B. SUMMERFORD (Private Secretary), PALGRAVE (Assistant Secretary), R. NELMES, HODGSON, MILLER, WHITE, LINDSELL, BUTLER, LEVY, APPERSON, HENDERSON, SLATER, GIBBS, HARVEY, and WRIGHT. } EDUCATION DEPARTMENT.

General WYNYARD.

J. R. DASENT, Esq., Private Secretary.

C. L. PEEL, Esq., C.B.

H. A. KINLOCH, Esq.

Dr. HOOD.

V. WING, Esq.

Mrs. MACNAGHTEN.

Mrs. RANDALL.

ROBERT ANDERSON, Esq., M.A.

M. P. MOLESWORTH, Esq.

WM. DEALTREY, Esq., C.M.G.

CONTENTS.

ERRATA.

Page 12. In the concluding phrase of last line, transpose, in reading, the words *stream* and *course*.

,, 28. In extract from "Childe Harold," for *contracted* read *contrasted*.

,, 32. In Foot-note (4) for Mocenigo read Morcenigo.

,, 33. In line 17, a dash — has been omitted before the words " the *vesta Zendale*."

,, 37. In the third Foot-note, the reference number (1) has been omitted.

,, 50, In line 12, for *time* read *crime*.

,, 59. In line 9, for *editor* read *Editor*.

,, 62. In fourteenth line from foot, for Mont*e* read Mont*i*.

,, 69. In eighth line from foot, for *exampes* read *examples*.

,, 71. In fifteenth line from foot, for *virgins* read *the virgins*.

,, 77. In seventeenth line from foot, at the end of the line, the final *t* has been omitted from *infrequent*.

N.B.—The small figures above the words in the text indicate foot-notes ; the larger figures refer to notes at the end, preceding the Appendix.

BIRTH AND CHILDHOOD OF LORD BYRON.

George Byron ([1]) was born in London ([2]), January 22nd, 1788, of a race illustrious by ancestry, but decayed in fortune (1). Have we to tell you of his boyhood? Obstinate, moody in temper, an obdurate enemy, adverse at first to study, then devoted to books (especially history,) at play eager, passionately fond of the beauties of nature—and, in particular of the sublime scenery of Scotland, where his mother left him, that in a keen air and with hardy exercise he might invigorate a feeble body—such was young Byron.

An uncle meanwhile died, and George, at ten years of age, found himself master and lord at Newstead Abbey. There, with a renowned title came those things, its concomitants, domestics, scholastic fame, the appellation of " my lord ;" and he demanded of his mother, " Have you discovered in me any difference since I have become a lord, for really I do not myself perceive it." The young peer took up his abode at Newstead (2), in Nottinghamshire, 136 miles from London, altogether without a care. And there, in idle tranquillity, he grew to youth under the mouldering tapestries of the old abbey ; amid boyish passions, at one time sad, at another gay, tho' why he knew not—passing in a moment from merriment to grief, from idleness to the most vigorous exercises. Dogs, horses, hunting and coursing, swimming, boxing, wrestling, and fencing, such were the occupations of the youthful peer. ·

Peel, who afterwards took so great a part in public affairs, was one day beaten with great cruelty by a bigger boy. Byron accosted the tyrant with indignation.

([1]). The baptismal names of Lord Byron were George Gordon Noel.
([2]). " Moore."—(It is believed in Holles street. Ed.) Mr. Dallas says "Dover."

B

"How much more do you intend giving him?" "What is that to you, you little rascal?" answered the other. "Because," replied Byron, "if you like, I will take half for him." Another schoolfellow, deformed in body, was subjected to derision and worse. "Harness," said Lord Byron, "if any one illtreats you, let me know, and I will thrash him if I can." And he kept his word. Boyish traits these, perhaps, but which, just because they are unnoticed by tutors, may become the germs of great actions.

II.

HIS FIRST POEMS.

The poetic fire was meanwhile developed in him, nor could be long undiscovered. At college, where he attended classes, his companions and masters perceived in the youth something extraordinary, and he himself felt born to fame. Seized with fits of deep melancholy, averse to any intercourse with his fellows, he would often seat himself on a tombstone in Harrow churchyard, and this his comrades called "Byron's Tomb." Here he wrote, "My epitaph (1), shall be my name alone."

Thus at 15 he wrote. Yet a little while, and, unable to restrain his boyish impatience, he gave to the world his first stanzas, "Hours of Idleness." Look not there for the great poet Childe Harold, but it would denote a want of perception of the beautiful, not to discover how great was the promise of these poems, some lines of which, as a sample and a picture of his youth, we cite. None, however, but the mountaineer by birth, or one whose first recollections and affections are thus associated, will enjoy their beauty.

> When I roved a young Highlander, o'er the dark heath,
>   And climb'd thy steep summit, oh, Morven, (1) of snow,
> To gaze on the torrent that thunder'd beneath,
>   Or the mist of the tempest that gather'd below ;
> Untutor'd by science, a stranger to fear,
>   And rude as the rocks where my infancy grew,
> No feeling save one, to my bosom was dear,
>   Need I say, my sweet Mary, t'was centred in you, &c. &c.

(1) An Ossianic expression—Morven is a mountain in Aberdeenshire.

These poems he published with the confident boldness of a youth who looks for applause, or at least encouragement.   Have you never experienced how bitter it is to receive instead censure and ridicule? This grief was Lord Byron's.   The *Edinburgh Review*, which, in its exemption from the routine of ordinary minds, instead of there discerning the beams of a bright intellect, discovered only the ravings of a degraded fancy, with impertinent irony tears to pieces these youthful poems, dissects them, analyses them with eye of lynx and heart of stone—treats the peer of England no otherwise than as a lad escaped from school, and of the future bard attempts to clip the wings.

"The poesy of this young Lord," says the *Review*, [1] "belongs to the class which neither men nor Gods are said to permit.   Indeed we do not recollect to have seen a quantity of verse with so few deviations in either direction from that exact standard.   His effusions are spread over a dead flat, and can no more get above or below the level than if they were so much stagnant water.   As an extenuation of this offence, the noble author is peculiarly forward in pleading minority . . . . .

" But alas, we all remember the poetry of Cowley at ten, and Pope at twelve ; and so far from hearing, with any degree of surprise, that very poor verses were written by a youth from his leaving school to his leaving college inclusive, we really believe this to be the most common of all occurrences ; that it happens in the life of nine men in ten who are educated in England, and that the tenth man writes better verse than Lord Byron. . . . . ." Oh! such a moment is for a youth the crisis of his life. Doubt it not.   If under the torture of his Mœvii (3), he succumbs, then adieu fame, adieu to study; he will abandon himself to idleness, to an indolent silence, useless if not noxious, to himself and others. Happy he who has sufficient strength of mind to acquire greater powers from opposition and the impulse to do better.

Long afterwards, Lord Byron said : " I recollect the effect on me of the *Edinburgh* on my first poem.   It was rage and resistance and redress—but not despondency

[1] *Edinburgh Review* of **January**, 1808.

B 2

nor despair.   I grant that those are not amiable feelings,
but, in this world of bustle and broil, and especially in the
career of writing, a man should calculate upon his powers
of *resistance* before he goes into the arena.

> "Expect not life from pain nor danger free,
> Nor deem the doom of man reversed for thee." (2)

In revenge, Byron wrote the "English Bards and Scotch
Reviewers," in which he tore to shreds the matured fame
of his country's writers.

His satire has all the *verve* of rage, he strikes friend
and foe ; you might compare him to a baited bull which
plunges amidst the crowd, trampling and goring without
distinction both his tormentors and the unoffending
spectators. England applauded the new Juvenal ; Byron
triumphed.   In after years he repented what he had
written, as is always the case with the writer of a
libel (4).

III.

LORD BYRON'S DISSIPATION.

But, before launching himself into the career of letters,
Byron had yet to go through a course of sensual enjoyment and of dissipation—riotous orgies where reason
became lost, duels for a trifle, a torn garment or a mis-
quoted verse.   Newstead Abbey was converted into a
scene of voluptuous delights.   There were the clearest
heads, the most renowned *bons vivans* of London ; there,
the first poets (?) of the day, the most courted actresses,
were assembled. Exquisite wines, delicious perfumes,
splendid illuminations, garlands of flowers, intertwined,
you might say, with dishevelled locks, convert the holy
cells of the monks into boudoirs most profane. And oh!
refectory, where still *silentium* remains inscribed, with
what toasts did thy walls resound !

"But if the place appear rather strange to you, the
ways of the inhabitants will not appear much less so.

(2) Letter to Shelley, Ravenna, April 26, 1821. *Moore's Life*, 1847,
p. 501.

Ascend then with me, the hall steps, that I may introduce you to my Lord and his visitants.   But have care
how you proceed; be mindful to go there in broad
daylight, and with your eyes about you.   For should
you make any blunder, should you go to the right
of the hall steps, you are laid hold of by a bear;
and should you go the left, your case is still worse,
for you run against a wolf!—nor, when you have
attained the door, is your danger over, for the
hall being decayed, and therefore standing in need of
repair, a bevy of inmates are probably hanging at one
end of it with their pistols, so that if you enter without
giving loud notice of your approach, you have only
escaped the wolf and the bear, to expire by the pistol
shots of the merry monks of Newstead (1). . . . . &c."

I must not omit the custom of handing round after
dinner, on the removal of the cloth, a human skull filled
with Burgundy.   Then, turning into mockery the
tradition of the dead, who, wrapped in funereal shroud,
arose as ghosts at midnight from their graves, these
jovial companions traversed the long corridors, disguised
as monks, and descending to the vaults, burst open the
sepulchres of the dead.   Nor then did they rise from
their unholy banquet until the sparkling Burgundy had
first gone round in a cup formed from a disentombed
skull.   On that skull the lines composed by Byron—who
adorned even his own *studio* with *crania* and skeletons, a
fantasy which some practice, as if fond not of being, but
of appearing, melancholy—were written :

> Start not, nor deem my spirit fled !
> In me behold the only skull,
> From which, unlike a living head, (2)
> Whatever flows is never dull."   &c.

Such were the orgies with which the poet prepared
himself for his appearance in Parliament, and his travels
in Greece and Italy.

IV.

APPEARS IN THE HOUSE OF LORDS.

In the House of Lords he presented himself alone, without a friend to introduce or welcome him, without a kinsman to motion him to a seat by his side. There, the interests of all Europe were then in discussion in connection with Napoleon, whose mind, gigantic as it ever was, had again turned to the overthrow of the factitious power of England. Most ardently desirous of instruction in the affairs of the country, Lord Byron there gave utterance to ideas too strange to that House, or that were then premature ; there, he at once with vehemence expressed the most liberal sentiments. How was he first received as a poet? With virulent censure. How in Parliament? With indifference, which is even worse (1). Discouraged, then, or unable in dissipation to stifle his chagrin, which arose from the collision betwixt the desire of action and impotence to act ; sated with the life of a wanderer at home, with an isolation amidst friends, mortified in his ambition at finding his wealth inadequate to his position, deceived in his first affections, he abandons his country, " a voluntary exile, fleeing his own heart."

V.

DEPARTURE FROM ENGLAND.

Scarcely on the ocean, the mighty ocean, whereon more especially than elsewhere the Deity has stamped the type of his power and of eternity, and again the poet revives.

> Adieu ! adieu ! my native shore (1)
> Fades o'er the waters blue ;
> The night winds sigh, the breakers roar,
> And shrieks the wild sea-mew.
> Yon sun that sets upon the sea,
> We follow in his flight ;
> Farewell alike to him and thee,
> My native land—good night ! &c.

(1) Childe Harold, Canto 1.

VI.

PORTRAIT OF LORD BYRON. (1.)

Whilst on his travels let us contemplate and sketch
the poet. He is handsome, and on his brow is read the
impress of an extraordinary mind. The predominating
characteristic of his countenance is an expression of
deep pensive meditation, which, in conversation, changes
to a rapid animation, on which follow in succession
flashes of joy, indignation, or satirical mirth. Rich
curls of luxuriant brown hair surround a spacious brow;
eyes of light blue sparkle with a brilliant fire; his cheek
is pale, but subsequently sunburned to a deeper hue;
the finest teeth—in fine, the whitest neck, shaped so
perfectly as to form a real model for the sculptor (1).
Of his good looks he was most careful, even indeed to
vanity. He never left his house but with hair and
person most carefully dressed, the finest linen, white as
snow, and clothes of the choicest materials; he used the
most exquisite perfumes, and took the most particular
care of his teeth. "The death of Waite," (2) he writes,
"is a shock to the teeth, as well as to the feelings of all
who knew him. Good God! he and Blake both (3) gone.
I left them both in the most robust health, and little
thought of the national loss in so short a time as five
years. . . . . Where is tooth powder, *mild* and yet
efficacious—where is *tincture*—where are cleaning roots
and brushes now to be obtained?" . . . . . Elsewhere he writes for tooth powder, magnesia, tincture of
myrrh, brushes, &c. In fact, in his dressing case might
have been found all the minute appurtenances of a lady's
toilet.

He took a singular pride in the extreme whiteness of
his hands; when he swam he wore gloves. He wrote to
his mother that the Pasha of Janina had told him that
he recognised him as a person of quality by the small-
ness of his ears, his curling hair, and his little white
hands (2). And elsewhere he says (3), "There is

(1) "His neck seemed to have been formed in a mould."—Madame T.
A., *Moore's Life.*

(2 and 3) Note to Stanza, 106. Don Juan, Canto 5.

nothing perhaps more distinctive of birth than the hand. It is almost the only sign of blood which aristocracy can generate."

It will be easy to surmise how dreadful to his mind must have been the defect of lameness in his feet, to which from his birth he was subject; and this was the greatest annoyance—one might almost say the deepest remorse—of his life. On that account was it that his clothes were always made long—that he generally rode on horseback, and went into society but little—while it may be affirmed that during the whole time he remained in Venice he scarcely went forth on foot, and never crossed the piazza of St. Mark (4), or entered its church. A deformity of this kind was ever before his eyes, so that in fact it appeared to him that this, rather than his good looks or his fame, drew upon him the public gaze. One day his friend Beecher, with the view of driving away the dejection which more than usually oppressed him, was setting forth in bright colours the various advantages wherewith Providence had endowed him. "Ah! my friend," mournfully responded Byron," if that (laying his hand on his forehead) places me above the rest of mankind, that (pointing to his foot) places me far below them " (4).

Another day he was on the course at Newmarket, and a little boy, addressing him by his title, offered him a standing chair. "You see," said Shelley to him, " you are so famous that even the boys on the course know you." "Yes," replied Byron, "because I am deformed" (5).

A tendency to flesh also displeased him greatly, and he tried every means to reduce himself (5). But the *embonpoint* to which he was inclined in no way interfered with his bodily activity, so that in every athletic exercise he was among the very first. "I am able," he afterwards wrote from Ravenna, in 1820, "to back a horse and fire a pistol without thinking or blinking like Major Sturgeon; I have fed at times for two months together on sheer biscuit and water (without metaphor); I can get over seventy or eighty miles a day *riding* post, and

---

(4) *Moore's Life*, 1847.
(5) Moore tells nearly the same anecdote, p. 357, Vol. I, 1830, of Byron and Rogers.

swim five at a stretch, as at Venice in 1818, or at least **I** *could* do, and have done it *once*." (⁶)

—————

VII.

LORD BYRON'S FAME.

Thus much for the body; as to the mind, throughout life it was actuated by three idols—fame, love, liberty. Whilst still a youth he gave forth his feelings in verse (¹).

> The fire in the cavern of Ætna concealed
> Still mantles unseen in its secret recess;
> At length, in a volume terrific revealed,
> No torrent can quench it, no bounds can repress.
>
> Oh! thus, the desire in my bosom for fame
> Bids me live but to hope for Posterity's praise;
> Could I soar, with the Phœnix, on pinions of flame,
> With him would I wish to expire in the blaze.
>
> In the life of a Fox, of a Chatham the death,
> What censure, what danger, what woe I would brave;
> Their lives did not end when they yielded their breath,—
> Their glory illumines the gloom of the grave! &c.

How many events were yet to harass this existence, and dispel so many illusions before he could write as follows, with sentiments so opposite (²).

> What is the end of fame, 'tis but to fill
> A certain portion of uncertain paper;
> Some liken it to climbing up a hill
> Whose summit, like all hills, is lost in vapour;
> For this men write, speak, preach, and heroes kill,
> And bards burn what they call their "midnight taper."
>   To have, when the original is dust—
>   A name, a wretched picture, and worse bust.

(6) *Moore's Life*, 1830, p. 379, Vol. II.—Letter to Mr. Murray.
(1) *Moore's Life*, 1830, p. 89.
(2) Don Juan, Canto 1.

VIII.

BYRON'S FIRST LOVE.

Love in him, like every other passion, was premature. He had not completed eight years when he became enamoured of Mary Duff. At about sixteen, the poet, after having been in love fifty times, recorded in impassioned verse the charms of Mary, her face, her brown dark hair, her hazel eyes, her very dress ([1]). Such precocious feelings will not surprise the countrymen of Dante and of Canova, of whom the former at nine became amorous of Beatrice, who was to lead him to Paradise ([2]), whilst the latter remembered a love passion at five years old ([3]). Alfieri anticipated the age of love, and describes its effects, which few understand and still fewer experience, but to how very few in all human arts is it permitted to leave behind the common crowd ([4]).

Afterwards, at twelve, his first verses were inspired by Miss Parker, his cousin, "one of the most beautiful of evanescent beings." "She looked," he wrote ([5]), "as if she had been made out of a rainbow—all beauty and peace" ([6]). She died about a year after ([7]). For three years nearly he lived fond to distraction of Mary Chaworth; it made him angry to see her dancing with another; he was in ecstasies when she touched the strings of her harp. But she was to wed another, and to him was she married (1).

Thus began the series of Byron's amours, which soon sadly persuaded him that love had nothing precious about it but its wings; and thus, through a host of transient passions, affording him no real happiness, we shall hereafter see him attached to an object more worthy of him.

(1, 2, 3, 4, 5, 6, 7,) *Moore's Life*, vol. 1, 2, pp. 17, 35, &c., &c.

IX.

TRAVELS IN SPAIN, ETC., ETC.

Liberty was his dream throughout his life's pilgrimage, from the day when he roved over the hills of Annesley, (¹) a giddy youth, until its final termination at Missolonghi. In pursuit of this, leaving the shores of England with Hobhouse, whom he ever held his dearest friend, he sailed over the ocean and the Mediterranean, and traversed Spain and Portugal, then beheld Greece, a land whose beauty, if not whose liberty or glory, lives yet intact; hailed the savage heights of Albania, the dark rocks of Suli, the stormy summits of Pindus, amidst whose recesses, undisturbed by song, dwell the eagle and wild animals, and still more ferocious men. With the " Albanian kirtled to his knee," " with shawl-girt sword and ornamented gun," he conversed, with the " crimson-scarfed men of Macedon," " the Delhi with his cap of terror and crooked glaive," " the lively, supple Greek," and " proud imperious Turk." There how great the diversity of mundane scenes and things within his ken; and the memorable field of Marathon is offered to him for ninety pounds sterling! Amid the groves, the fabled abode of nymphs, in the harmonious recesses where sang the muses, shall not the lyre of Byron again awake? Hark! What strain of melodious song is heard? Perchance the vocal harmony of the poets who, as in more joyous days, to the sound of lyres intone the praises of the Olympian conquerors, or of him who put to rout the Persian hosts! It is the harp of the English bard which pours forth the vigorous song of beauty and of valour. (²)

> Fair clime! where every season smiles
> Benignant o'er those blessed isles,
> Which, seen from far Colonna's height,
> Make glad the heart that hails the sight,
> And lend to loneliness delight, &c., &c.

(¹) The residence of the Chaworths, and scene of passages in the Dream," one of his *chefs d'œuvres.*
(²) The Giaour.

X.

CHILDE HAROLD'S PILGRIMAGE.

How long had it been declared that poetry had passed away, that the epic lyre had lost its sound! And, lo! amid the turmoil of Europe, disturbed by the restless genius of Napoleon, appeared a poem, at once an Iliad and an Odyssey, a poem which stands alone in our age, which might yet have furnished subjects for so many poems. Ancient poetry no longer lived. A stroke of imagination and a touch of style were ingredients enough for the day to form a poet. A poet resided at Court, was a member of the magistracy, owned houses and property, possessed friends and family; as other men he rose and slept, and, whilst luxuriously reclining, in dressing gown arrayed, before his fire, withdrew from the walls his disused lyre, and wrote an epic according to the rules of Aristotle—a *vade mecum* of the true sublime—imagining men, costumes, laws, countries, names, portraying then the whole with the marvels of antiquated beliefs, neither true nor even credible.

The Æneid, a poem of Italian antiquity, was written under the smiling sky of Calabria, or at the Augustan Court, perfuming the monarch with the incense which impairs so much the vivid colouring of that divine poem. Arisoto wrote his verses often when seated at the table of the Duke, (1) "betwixt the latter and Lucrezia Borgia, or after kissing the Pope's feet, or whilst governing Garfagnana, (2), amid accusations and law pleadings. Little otherwise was composed the Henriade, (3). Telemachus was written through a translation (4). And Tasso, of whose name the city of his birth is so justly proud, sought not the sacred scenes for truth or inspiration, or the hills and woods mindful of the muses of song famed in Helicon, "but thus, from a height above Ferrara, addressed his invocation: See ye these fields, these Campaniles, these streams, this people! Behold! there is my poem!"

In juxtaposition with these regard Homer: limping along, step by step, all Greece he visited; he knew its every path, its smallest hill, of every course the stream he traced, from every part he gathered the dialogue, in his tongue to be immortalized ; he suffers want for bread, and begs through the cities, afterwards to dispute the honour of his cradle. Behold the Homer of the Middle Ages, Dante, (¹) exiled, condemned to die, who wields a patriot's arms, who, leaving all he cherished most, goes from land to land, experiencing how bitter is the bread of strangers. He reposes in a convent, asking peace from the Church, he seeks instruction in the fine Tuscan tongue, and, a traveller thro' all cities, in none reposes. Thus genius rises amidst difficulties, thus emerge the great whom then the world adores.

And a poet such as this did Byron wish to be. Already all that in the belief of men and in fiction could inspire a poet was lost; the destructive hand of the Revolution had torn away all the veils of Isis but the last, and that removed, a carcase was revealed ; and a cry, which, under Tiberius, had already resounded over the seas, had announced—the Gods are dead ! Meantime, the exercise of thought, more active than ever, had become a passion, nay, a torment—the progress of knowledge, the daily discoveries, the more rapid events of history, more stupendous than the fancy could have imagined, demanded other poets and other hearers, a poetry inspired, effective, equal to the impulsion which portentous events had communicated to men's minds. No longer were desired descriptions at caprice, nor imaginary heroes, ideal, shadow-like, nor conventional discourses, but truth ; the true, perfected in action, seen and felt. It had become necessary to penetrate the innermost recesses of man's mind, to reveal his passions, to lay bare his heart. This would Byron do. The age that had said to Cooper, "Tell me of the sea ;" to Walter Scott, "Paint me Scotland ;" said to Byron, "Speak to me of thyself. Reveal to me a mind above the crowd ; be thou thyself thine own Achilles, thy own Godfrey ; or when thou speakest not of thyself, relate to me what thou hast thyself seen."

Byron understood this, and gave himself to the study of man's destruction ; of nature and art's decay ; contemplated man contending no longer with giants or with gods but with his own passions, with anguish, with death. He

(1) Dante was condemned, first, to confiscation of all his property ; secondly, to be burned alive.—Ed. and Translator.

meditated on himself; and melancholy, if already · it had before inspired at times his verse, was by him invoked as his only muse.

This was it that dictated for him the Pilgrimage of Childe Harold, the narrative of his travels, from whence returned, he scarcely, or with difficulty, found a printer for his verse. Yet a little while, and every line was purchased at a guinea. Rarely had so powerful a voice been heard amid the feeble tones of those the so-called great writers of the day, and the old generation revolted against a novelty or an innovation it comprehended not. The age coming, or to come, found it adapted to its understanding. In short, admiration gained the day; Childe Harold appeared the most natural production of the age. All strove to praise the author, all desired to gain his friendship. "I awoke," he wrote, "one morning and found myself famous." (²).

And the *Edinburgh Review!* Not even could this gainsay his title to fame; but it would still affirm that the marvels which so delighted the world were void or all which usually pleases and attracts.

XI.

CONTEMPORARY POETS.

The scene on which the poet had with such brilliancy just appeared, was worthy of his greatness. England, itself astounded at having overthrown the Colossus which held the dagger to her breast, at having entered in triumph the Metropolis of the French Empire, whilst it restored order to Europe by arms and gold, was likewise insinuating the essence of its spirit into foreign literature. Hundreds of new celebrities arose. Crabbe, young and free from care or want, had entered the lists of song. Lewis had thrown down the gauntlet to the most impassioned lovers of the terrible. Coleridge was

(²) Memoranda.—*Moore's Life.*

preparing all the powers of a thoughtful imagination, which he then abandoned to a careless indolence. Canning, still a youth, was proving in satire the eloquence which was afterwards to give him sway in Parliament and a premature end. Campbell, already supreme in didactics, had promised himself fresh triumphs in Odes, and "was the only contemporary poet," said Byron, "who could be reproached with having written too little." (¹). Thomas Moore, with a style thoroughly brilliant, had transplanted to England the fairy tales of the East. Rogers brought back to remembrance the harmony of Pope. Wordsworth, if at times childish—if (as Byron, somewhat disposed against him, declared) he placed a *dyke* between his own intellect and others, had yet learned to wield a language magnificent as the scenes he contemplated. Southey, the constant butt for the raillery of Byron, by dint of intellect, imagination, grace, and style, was sustaining the fame of the old school, or, as it was styled, the Lake School (²). But above the others soared Walter Scott, who, drawing his models from the middle ages, and reviving the minstrels, had ascended to the pinnacle of poetic fame, and was soon about to rise, if possible, still higher as a novelist.

By different paths Scott and Byron aspired to fame. The former varied to infinity his characters; the latter produced again and again the same, changing somewhat perhaps the outlines. The first describes the dress and contour of the person and countenance; the second analyses the mind. The former, of a landscape or of a mansion will give you a topography or description that might enable you to sketch it with your pencil; the latter studies the inhabitants and their passions. Walter Scott ponders well the choice of his subject; to Byron anything and everything is alike a theme. Scott is more picturesque, Byron more impassioned; in the first is more of order and symmetry; in the second, more of impetuosity and inspiration.

The romance writer thus depicted the poet :—" It was in the spring of 1815 that, chancing to be in London, I

(¹) Except Rogers.—See *Moore's Life*, p. 444, 1847.
(²) See dictionary of 10,000 living English writers, of whom 1,987 are poets.

had the advantage of a personal introduction to Lord Byron. Report had prepared me to meet a man of peculiar habits and a quick temper, and I had some doubts whether we were likely to suit each other in society. I was most disagreeably disappointed in this respect. I found Byron in the highest degree courteous and even kind. We met for an hour or two almost daily in Mr. Murray's drawing-room, and found a great deal to say to each other. We also met frequently in parties and evening society, so that for about two months I had the advantage of a considerable intimacy with this distinguished individual. Our sentiments agreed a good deal, except upon the subjects of religion and politics, upon neither of which I was inclined to believe that Lord Byron entertained very fixed opinions. I remember saying to him that I really thought that if he lived a few years longer he would alter his sentiments. He answered, rather sharply, ' I suppose you are one of those who prophecy I will turn Methodist ! ' I replied, " No, I don't expect your conversion to be of such an ordinary kind. I would rather look to see you retreat upon the Catholic faith, and distinguish yourself by the austerity of your penances (1). The species of religion to which you must, or may, attach yourself must exercise a strong power on the imagination. He smiled gravely, and seemed to allow I must be right. On politics he used sometimes to express a high strain of what is now called Liberalism ; but it appeared to me that the pleasure it afforded him as a vehicle of displaying his wit and satire against individuals in office, was at the bottom of this habit of thinking, rather than any real conviction of the political principles on which he talked. He was certainly proud of his rank and ancient family, and in that respect as much an aristocrat as was consistent with good sense and good breeding. Some disgusts, how adopted I know not, seemed to me to have given rise to this peculiar, and, as it appeared to me contradictory cast of mind ; but, at heart, I would have termed Byron a patrician on principle. Lord Byron's reading does not seem to have been very extensive, either in poetry or history. Having the advantage of him in that respect, and possessing a good competent share of such reading as is little read, I was sometimes able to put under his eye objects which had for him the interest of novelty."

Subsequent to this year (1815), Scott never saw Byron again, but he continues :—" Several letters passed between us—one perhaps every half-year. Like the old heroes in Homer, we exchanged gifts—I gave Byron a beautiful dagger, mounted with gold, which had been the property of the renowned Elfi Bey. But I was to play the part of Diomed in the *Iliad*; for Byron sent me some time after a large sepulchral vase of silver. It was full of dead men's bones, and had inscriptions on two sides of the vase. One ran thus:—' The bones contained in this urn were found in certain ancient sepulchres within the land walls of Athens in the month of February, 1811.' The other face bears the lines of Juvenal (³) :—

> Expende—quot libras in duce summo invenies.
> Mors sola fatetur quantula minimum corpuscula.'

Byron was often melancholy. . . . . almost gloomy. When I observed him in this humour, I used rather to wait till it went off of its own accord, or till some natural and easy mode occurred of leading him into conversation, when the shadows almost always left his countenance like the mists arising from a landscape. In conversation he was very animated. . . . . I think I also remarked in Byron's temper starts of suspicion, when he seems to pause and consider whether there had not been a secret and perhaps offensive meaning in something casually said to him. In this case I also judged it best to let his mind, like a troubled spring, work itself clear, which it did in a minute or two. I was considered older, you will recollect, than my noble friend, and had no reason to fear his misconstruing my sentiments towards him, nor had I ever the slightest reason to doubt that they were kindly returned on his part. If I had occasion to be mortified by the display of genius which threw into the shade such pretensions as I was then supposed to possess, I might console myself that in my own case the materials of mental happiness had been mingled in greater proportion. I rummage my

(3) X. 4. (See also heading to the "Ode to Napoleon.")

C

brains in vain for what often rushes into my head
unbidden—little traits and sayings which recall his looks,
manner, tone, and gestures; and I have always continued to think that a crisis of his life was arrived, in
which a new career of fame was opened to him, and
that had he been permitted to start upon it, he would
soon have obliterated the memory of such parts of his
life as friends would wish to forget. (⁴) .   .   .   .''

With still more of heart did Byron speak of Walter
Scott:—'' I have never met with any one with the same
power of making me forget my own troubles, and with-
draw my thoughts from myself.   After passing some
time with Walter Scott I felt myself again restored to
youth, and relieved of a heavy burthen.   To him only,
perhaps, can I be under obligations for having aroused
within me the feelings of unalloyed enjoyment, unmingled
with bitterness.'' (⁵).

Such then were the contemporaries amongst whom Byron
pursued his way to fame, with the applause of friends,
and the tacit consent of enemies.   A style rich in thought
and imagery, a vivifying power over all that came to his
hand—a creative combination or grouping, altogether
new, and the awakening of emotions till then unknown,
caused a greedy rush for his works, which yet seemed
directly opposed to the doctrines most commonly received.   At first, the passions he depicted seemed to the
reader contrary to truth, but, diving deeper into the heart
of man, we there at last find their truth, though at the
outset neither perceived nor sought. Strangely it flattered
us to find ourselves identified with the poet, with such a
poet, living with his breath, respiring with his greatness
only, carried along by the vortex of his thoughts.

XII.

THE CORSAIR AND OTHER TALES.

Filled with the inspirations of the East—that then un-
trodden region, and the which Goethe and Moore, Hugo

(⁴ and ⁵). Life of Walter Scott. *Moore's Life of Byron*, 1847.

and Lamartine had also then imbibed—from thence Byron
drew also the subject of many poems. Zuleika, The
Corsair, The Giaour, the Siege of Corinth—you might
style them all exquisite pictures tapestried upon the same
canvas. Throughout all we have a man, heroic only in
resolution or in misdeeds and peril; for his virtue, pride;
his only human sentiment, love, but this of fire, and to
excess and to exaggeration. "Oh! youth," exclaims
Nodier, "treasure up your love; it is the divinity of
your age." We have ourselves often felt that it is time
to give over depicting the passion of love, and that this
age, ever more greedy of the truth and of utility, is
weary of such strains. But, since the passion of love is
the sentiment the most general amongst men; since
from it arise most follies and most fine actions; since
from it we see poets, even, the greatest of every clime
and age, select their theme, why seek to proclaim a law
of exclusion which, like all things unreasonable, will
certainly be infringed? Nor should we strive to extin-
guish the passions. They are the natural consequences
of our nature, but let them be directed by reason, and to
a good end.

Therefore has the writer of these pages congratulated
himself, albeit in youthful verse, at having got rid of
those ever-recurring strains of love wherewith Arcadians
and Petrarchists have wearied the ears and cajoled the
public imagination, nor yet believes it a reflection on
him who makes of love the moving spring of tragedy and
romance. Why not, in fact, if it be the moving spring
of real life? Or has, perchance, the greatest of living
poets desired to be untrammelled by it? And here
would this same writer wish his voice had power to
make itself heard, that he might exhort the youth of
Italy not to be deluded into following the models of
those, particularly among the French, who know not
how to divest their love-scenes of the most exuberant
exaggeration, and crimes, and convulsions.

Oh! is not woman the most attractive ornament in
our state of being? Do we not owe to her the content-
ments of our childhood, of which, through life, we retain
the soothing recollection? Is not with woman the most
delicious moments of our youth? Is not with woman our

consolation in our troubles; the relief of our maladies? But woman, we would say, with her most prominent characteristics, modesty and sweetness of temper, (1) to be loved and esteemed as she deserves. Who otherwise depicts her travesties her ideality equally with him who brings her out a strolling player in the public square, a dancer on the tight-rope, or an equestrian in the circus.

Neither shall we lament over the perpetual *couleur de rose* wherewith poets from time immemorial have tinged their sweet measures, of which we know but the golden locks, eyes tremulous with love, and the *tout ensemble* of an insipid face reprinted on the inanimate profile of Laura. But that of Herminia, who, on the bark of the beech and the laurel, carves the cherished name in endless forms of love, is an image that we prefer, We love, too, the meditative Julia on Lake Leman's shores, and fearful not so much of the love of her beloved, as of her own.

We love in Rinaldo, the Amelia, who, from nature, had received divine and indescribable attractions: "her mind possessed the same ingenuous graces as her person; exquisite sweetness of thought, and in her disposition all that was delightful and likewise pensive. She possessed the timidity and love of woman, and the purity and harmony of the angels." The Lauretta and Theresa of Ortis likewise must please, and the Laura of Manzoni, who, you may say, perhaps, could neither love nor hate, and we reply—she is true to life—she is nature.

This digression on our part will appear perhaps only useless to those who have not discovered in every-day literature a tendency to caricature, to exaggeration, which, if the well-disposed will not oppose, much evil may result to letters and the sacred characteristics of beauty, truth, and civilization, which they are destined to perfect ! No ! Italian fancy, guided ever only by a calm and truthful observation, never, we trust, will consent to place woman amid scenes of horror and revenge, amidst villanies, and beside its concomitant, the executioner, as are wont to do the highest intellects of another nation, but to whom can certainly accrue neither fame nor advantage from such disordered fantasies [1]. Ah! sad is that man's fate who, in the craving for strong emotions, knows only how to recover himself on the bed of sin, or at the foot of the scaffold!

But to such a school would ever have given encouragement the poet of whom we speak? Alas! too truly we believe it; although perhaps little otherwise than Tasso contributed to deprave the taste of the *Sei-cento*. Certain enough is it that Byron strives to excite emotion, to sway by his genius the imagination of his reader, without caring for the moral consequences; that he even makes a vaunt of inspiring us with sympathy for beings with whom we never wish conformity of sentiment. He always considers women solely under the aspect of the passion of love, and not in their individuality, from whence it is they are not portrayed as natural and true, but fashioned by his taste and caprice.

In the Siege of Corinth (2), the Venetian Alp, a renegade who, through animosity, abjured his country and his faith, himself leads the Turks to the siege of Corinth, in which is then beleaguered the Christian damsel whom he loves. And she, Francesca, visits him to persuade him to become a convert, in vain (3). The next day Alp attacks and takes the city. He encounters Minotti, the father of his beloved, and as he hears from his lips that she is dead, and that her spirit alone had appeared to him, he leaves his breast unguarded to the death wound, whilst Minotti, setting fire to the magazine, buries himself and his enemies under the ruins of the captured city.

Lara is enveloped altogether in mystery, into the abyss of which the imagination of the reader does not penetrate; mysterious crimes torment him with remorse, the secret and remedy of which is known only to his Page (4).

The Corsair was perhaps a man of virtuous instincts, but circumstances have made him the leader of a band of pirates; have rendered him an enemy of the human race; greedy of fame, but unable to acquire it by great actions, he seeks it in the savage indulgence of revenge

(1) The writings of the famous Balzac, the not less famous Victor Hugo, Borel, and others, are here referred to.—Ed.

and destruction, until he dies a man " of one virtue and a thousand crimes." (²).

Love and hatred form the existence of the Giaour.

> My days, though few, have passed below
> In much of joy, but more of woe;
> Yet still in hours of love and strife,
> I've 'scaped the weariness of life;
> Now leagued with friends, now girt by foes,
> I loathed the languor of repose,
> Now nothing left to love or hate,
> No more with hope or pride elate.
>
> But place again before my eyes,
> Aught that I deem a worthy prize;
> The maid I love, the man I hate,
> And I will hunt the steps of fate,
> To save or slay, as these require,
> Through rending steel and rolling fire, &c.

Here throughout we find again an intensity of grief and of desire, whence gush forth violent passions that, amidst the smiling scenes where they occur, assimilate the poet to a volcano, when, over the verdant landscape, it vomits forth ashes and stones and torrents of lava. Here, however, we have not the truth pictured but rather an ideal, a study, in fact, which materially deviates from the natural and true.

Nor is it the duty of the poet who knows perfectly his vocation to cause undue emotion, or disturb the mind's tranquility, or transport it to a sphere beyond the limits of nature, even be it one of virtue, but from which, descending or expelled, it wanders guideless; rather should he design to develop the moral powers, so that by his instrumentality the passions may be governed or truly directed.

XIII.

BYRON'S MARRIAGE.

Amidst such scenes Byron abandoned not the reckless habits of his youth, until at last he himself felt the

(2) The Corsair.

craving for domestic happiness, and sought a wife,—
Byron a wife! To put his house in order, send away
his dogs, horses, monkeys, pay off his debts, arrange his
books—no display henceforth of pistols or of foils—
sheathed must be his Albanian scimitar—no longer his
aspect or appearance that of one inspired! He chooses
a tranquil moment, and demands as his wife the daughter
of Sir Ralph Milbank Noel, heiress to the title and
revenues of the Wentworths ; leads her to the altar, and
promises himself a happy and domestic life (1). But
what if the man of pleasure should again appear? If
the poet should again revive? If the sated youth, the
melancholy dreamer, the adventurous Harold, should
again return? Where then the husband, the father?

And thus it came to pass. That felicity—how happy
he who enjoys it!—was not for Byron's mind: the
caresses of a wife, the smiles of an infant, of which
a year after he was the fortunate father, the
tranquillity of the domestic hearth, were not to
relax the poetical sinews of a mind strained by real
or fancied wrongs. What and how much has not
been said of the unforeseen and mysterious separation
of Lord Byron from his wife! A day comes, and she
goes to her father's house on the pretext of a visit, and
thence writes to her husband that she will never return
to him. We do not attempt to lose ourselves in a
labyrinth of accusations and retorts: it has been said
that great men should be admired, but cannot be loved ;
we, however, who are acquainted with Romagnosi (2)
and Manzoni (3), we say, that this is the plea of men
too petty and too malicious, of those, too numerous,
alas! who cannot forgive him who raises himself above
the crowd (4), and who may be compared to the disin-
herited, whose hatred or virulence would seize or keep
back the property of their brethren.

The excessive expenditure entailed by espousing a
wealthy heiress; the continual claims of creditors,
carried to the seizure of property and furniture (5) ; the
fact of being watched in his own house, and out
of doors ; the existence of domestic disorder excluding
Lord Byron almost from society; the self-imposed duty
of maintaining acquaintance with actresses (6) ; all this,

combined with an essential difference of habits and disposition between a rich heiress desirous of living as a great lady and a man of genius who was willing neither to rule in his own house nor be ruled; all this, fomented by the perfidious suggestions of the lady's companion or governess(¹)—was it not enough to explain the discord between both? Where, in fact, the marvel that a marriage arranged by calculations of rank and of opinions (or of *convenance*) without regard to the heart's affections and sympathy of disposition and inclinations, should turn out ill? Is it not daily the case?

But the English, with whom marriage occupies a position so different from that it holds with us; the English, who so frequently are witnesses of the recurrence of scandalous trials where witnesses are cited who have listened by the nuptial couch, or spied through the bath door, and who testify exactly how much and what they saw and heard; the English, who fix a tariff for payment of such injuries, could never pardon Byron for separating from his wife (7) without assigning a cause, without appearing in court to satisfy the greed of the lawyers and the curiosity of the public. They, therefore, vented their spleen in satirical *on dits*, in caricatures, in charging the poet with every possible kind of phrenzy and misdeed (²). "My case was supposed to comprise all the crimes which could, and several which could not, be committed, and little less than an *auto-da-fè* was anticipated as the result (8). But let no man say that we are abandoned by our friends in adversity—it was just the reverse. Mine thronged around me to condemn, advise, and console me with their disapprobation. They told me all that was, would, or could be said on the subject. They shook their heads—they exhorted me—deplored me, with tears in their eyes, and—went to dinner."

And yet how meanly was the posthumous work, which should have revealed the whole affair, denied to public expectation. All who have read the poetry of

(1) Mrs. Clermont (or Charlemont) whom he anathematizes in the sketch from private life.
(2) *Moore's Life*, 1830, p. 522, Vol. 2.

Byron well know how affectionately he often recurs to his wife.

> Fare thee well ! and if for ever,
>   Still for ever, fare *thee well* :
> E'en though unforgiving, never
>   'Gainst thee shall my heart rebel.
> Would that breast were bared before thee,
>   Where thy head so oft hath lain ;
> While that placid sleep came o'er thee,
>   Which thou ne'er canst know again !
> Would that breast, by thee glanced over,
>   Every inmost thought could show !
> Then thou wouldst at last discover
>   'Twas not well to spurn it so.
> Though the world for this commend thee,
>   Though it smile upon the blow ;
> E'en its praises must offend thee,
>   Founded on another's woe. &c., &c.

This poem, which drew from Madame de Stael (3) the expression "I would willingly suffer what Lady Byron has done, to have inspired my husband with such beautiful verse," moved not the lady. The lyre of Orpheus will soften the pangs of hell, but not the heart of a proud woman. Had she not otherwise been wrong, we would not forgive her for having refused forgiveness to a husband who asked it, and such a husband. Such conduct could not but embitter his lot, and here we would introduce two compositions wherein is revealed the anguish of his mind. When, in 1816, he learned that Lady Byron was ill, it grieved him much, and he threw into the fire a satirical romance founded on the well-known story of Belphegor, but he afterwards wrote a poem (9) of which the prudence of Moore gave us only the first verses, but which is now usually published entire.

> And thou wer't sad—yet I was not with thee !
>   And thou wer't sick, and yet I was not near ;
> Methought that joy and health alone could be
>   Where I was not—and pain and sorrow here ! &c.

In 1821, from Pisa, he thus wrote to his wife :—

Pisa, Nov. 17, 1821.

I have to acknowledge the receipt of Ada's hair, which is very soft and pretty, and nearly as dark already as mine was at 12 years old, if I may judge from what I recollect of some in Augusta's possession, taken at that age. But it don't curl—perhaps from its being let grow. I also thank you for the inscription of the date and name ; and I will tell you why ; I believe they are the only two or three words of your hand-

(3) Madame de Stael (See Memoirs).

writing in my possession; for your letters I returned, and except the two words, or rather the one word, "Household," written twice in an old account book, I have no other.   I burnt your last note, for two reasons—firstly, as it was written in a style not very agreeable; and secondly, I wished to take your word without documents, which are the worldly resources of suspicious people.

I suppose that this note will reach you somewhere about Ada's birth-day—the 10th of December, I believe.   She will then be six, so that in about twelve more, I shall have some chance of meeting her—perhaps sooner if I am obliged to go to England by business or otherwise. Recollect, however, one thing, either in distance or otherwise ; every day which keeps us asunder should, after so long a period, rather soften our mutual feelings, which must always have one rallying point as long as our child exists, which I presume we both hope will be long after either of her parents.

The time which has elapsed since the separation has been consider-ably more than the whole brief period of our union, and the not much longer one of our prior acquaintance.   We both made a bitter mistake, but now it is over, and irrecoverably so.   For, at 33 on my part, and a few years less on yours, though it is no very extended period of life, still it is one when the habits and thoughts are generally so formed as to admit of no modification; and as we could not agree when younger, we should with difficulty do so now.   I say all this because I own to you that, notwithstanding everything, I considered our re-union as not im-posible for more than a year after the separation; but then, I gave up the hope entirely and for ever.   But this very impossibility of re-union seemed to me at least a reason why, on all the few points of discussion which can arise between us, we should preserve the courtesies of life, and as much of its kindness as people who are never to meet may preserve perhaps more easily than nearer connections.   For my own part, I am violent, but not malignant, for only fresh provocations can awaken my resentments.

To you, who are colder and more concentrate, I would just hint that you may sometimes mistake the depth of a cold anger for dignity and a worse feeling for duty.   I assure you that I bear you *now* (whatever I may have done) no resentment whatever.

Remember that *if you have injured me* in aught, this forgiveness is something; and that if I have *injured you*, it is something more still, if it be true, as the moralists say, that the most offending are the least forgiving.

Whether the offence has been solely on my side, or reciprocal, or on yonrs chiefly, I have ceased to reflect upon any but two things—viz. : that you are the mother of my child and that we shall never meet again. I think if you also consider these two corresponding points with reference to myself it will be better for all three.—Yours ever,

NOEL BYRON.

XIV.

LORD BYRON AGAIN LEAVES ENGLAND.

Thus wrote the man whom the fops of London, affected young ladies, and exclusive society there—offended with his plain speaking and undisguised contempt—would, with an hypocritical affectation of honourable feeling, have exposed as a monster to the horror of the married world. Proud islanders! Their trivial prating, so much the more tiresome since it was masked by gravity, wearied the mind of Byron, who, too great a poet to become a philosopher, could not oppose a heart hardened to the wounds of malice, the storm of libels, verses, journals, and caricatures of which he became the object, and which are an unfortunate concomitant of the more vaunted than real liberty of his country. Therefore had he declared himself subdued; and, departing from his home—his home no more, for without the heart's affection there is no home (1)—he broke all ties which yet bound him to his natal soil (April 25, 1816); again he bids adieu to his native land and his child, and departs to return no more.

> Is thy face like thy mother's, my fair child? (2)
> Ada! sole daughter of my house and heart;
> When late I saw thy young blue eyes, they smiled,
> And when we parted,—not as now we part,
> But with a hope—&c. . . . . I depart.

> Whither I know not, ...
> I see thee not,—I hear *thee not, but* none
> Can be so wrapt up in thee; . . .
> Albeit my brow thou never shouldst behold,
> My voice shall with thy future visions blend,
> And reach into thy heart,—when mine is cold;—
> A token and a tone, e'en from thy father's mould.

> To aid thy mind's development,—to watch
> Thy dawn of little joys—to sit and see—
> Almost thy very growth,—to view thee catch
> Knowledge of objects,—wonders yet to thee!
> To hold thee lightly on a gentle knee,
> And print on thy soft cheek a parent's kiss—
> This, it should seem, was not reserved for me;
> Yet this was in my nature,—as it is,
> I know not what is there, yet something like to this.
> . . . .

(1) Don Juan, Canto 3.
(2) Childe Harold, Canto 3.

XV.

TRAVELS OF LORD BYRON.

An exile from his country, without the consolation of the martyr, discontented with himself and those about him, and at war with the world, which he fancied he could do without, behold him again the poet, the head-strong, sombre, pensive poet, and regard the poetry he is writing and which he shall hereafter write.

He visits the field of Waterloo, trampling on the dust of a great empire; from Belgium to Coblenz, thence to Switzerland, where he visits the field of Morat, one of the few sites where man can contemplate the horrid trophies of victory without feeling shame for the victors; climbs to the Dent de Jarman, traverses the Rhine, sails along the lakes, converses with Madame de Stael, searches for traces of the memory of Voltaire, of Rousseau, of Gibbon, and amid the woods, still mindful of the melancholy loves of the "Nouvelle Heloise," composes the "Prisoner of Chillon." The tranquil innocence of the landscape here is soothing to his stormy but wearied spirit.

> Clear placid Leman, thy contracted lake, (1)
>   With the wild world I dwelt in, is a thing
> Which warns me with its stillness to forsake
>   Earth's troubled waters for a purer spring.
>   .   .   .   .
>
> Here the self-torturing sophist, wild Rousseau,
>   The apostle of affliction, he who threw
> Enchantment over passion, and from woe
>   Wrung overwhelming eloquence, first drew
>   The breath which made him wretched; yet who
> Knew how to make madness beautiful, and cast
>   O'er erring deeds and thoughts a heavenly hue
> Of words, like sunbeams, dazzling as they passed
> The eyes, which o'er them shed tears feelingly and fast.
>   .   .   .   .
>
> His life was one long war with self-sought foes,
>   Or friends by himself banish'd; for his mind
> Had grown suspicion's sanctuary, and chose
>   For its own cruel sacrifice the kind
> 'Gainst whom he raged with fury, strange and blind,
> But he was frenzied,—wherefore, who may know?
>   .   .   .   .   &c.

(1) Childe Harold, Canto 3.

However often Byron would deny the resemblance said to exist between himself and the Genevese (1), we must yet confess that in many points they were strangely akin in their egotism, and in the effect they produced on others ; in the exaggeration also of their own misfortunes, governed by which sentiment the young lord flies his native land, everywhere dragging along with him his antipathy to his wandering countrymen, in whose presence he everywhere finds himself. He meets them on the field of Waterloo, purchasing fragments of French arms and speculating in the bones of the unburied. At Rome he sees them hurrying past the masterpieces for which the study of a day should scarce suffice. In Switzerland, at one of those stupendous prospects, never effaced from the mind of him who once has contemplated them, he encountered a family of these new-fashioned gipsies, who, were journeying whilst asleep in their travelling *calèche*. He met them trafficking even amidst the ruins of Athens, where Lord Elgin, proud of having robbed Greece of those memorials of art the barbarians had spared, carved his name on a column of a ruined temple, a column which still proudly towers, a remnant amidst the sacred dust of ancient freedom—an outrage, however, which the poet avenged by erasing that name with his own hand. A little later, and he will again meet them in awakened Greece, when, asked for arms and bread, they offer music and band instruments.

Thenceforth, the poet wanted no motive for exasperation against them, and one might say lived in a perpetual abnegation of the land of his birth. Hence the affectation of hatred of his countrymen, which was refuted by his hospitality towards them. Hence no longer was cele- brated in song his native isle, the favourite or usual theme of British poets. Hence strove he to rob them of the laurels acquired in Spain and at Waterloo. Hence spontaneously he rose to denounce the atrocious selfish- ness wherewith nations sell and thus betray the new Themistocles, who came a suppliant for their hospitality, and found chains on the land that claims to be hospitable and free (2).

Hence why, even in his style of writing, he followed not

(2) The author's rather than the editor's sentiments !

any of the English classic writers, but composed with a mixture of bitterness and grace, negligence and precision, gravity and mockery, which might perhaps find a parallel only in the "Pulci" of Ariosto, in Dante, or other Italian poets.

XVI.

ITALY.

The land and ashes of these bards he came to mourn over, to venerate that lovely Italy, which now, for the fourth time, held its pre-eminence in the world, the primacy of power with the Romans—that of religion under the Popes,—that of commerce with the Republics—and lastly that of arts and learning.

Descending the Simplon, where he regards with wonder both nature and art (1), one can scarcely say which the most stupendous, he visits the charming delights of Lago Maggiore. Thence, in Milan, admires the wonders of the Duomo, and the courtesy of the inhabitants (2); at Garda he contemplates the Benaco (3) surging with the noise of the sea; at Verona, so many recollections of love and grandeur.

Then he descends the Po, and amidst the wide and grassworn streets of Ferrara, indites a sonnet to the good Torquato, whose name finds everywhere an echo of applause in this Athenæum of his country:

> Hail to the bard divine⁻ . . . .
>   Hark to the strain : and then survey his cell !
> And see how dearly earned Torquato's fame,
>   And where Alphonso bade his poet dwell !"
> *   *   *   *   *   *
> Peace to Torquato's injured shade ! 'twas his
>   In life and death to be the mark where wrong
> Aim'd with his poisoned arrows but to miss.

He then passes to the happy banks of the Arno and to Rome, the "Niobe of nations;" at length repairs to

Venice, of all places but the East the most courted
of his fancy ([1]) :

> I stood in Venice, on the Bridge of Sighs :
>   A palace and a prison on each hand ;
> I saw from out the wave her structures rise,
>   As from the stroke of the Enchanter's Wand ;
> A thousand years their cloudy wings expand
>   Around me, and a dying glory smiles
> O'er the far times, when many a subject land
>   Looked to the wingéd Lion's marbled piles,
>   Where Venice sat in state, throned on her hundred Isles !
>
> She looks a Sea-Cybele, fresh from ocean ;
>   Rising, with her tiara of proud towers
> At airy distance, with majestic motion,
>   A ruler of the waters and their powers.
> And such she was,—her daughters had their dowers
>   From spoils of nations ; and the exhaustless East
> Poured in her lap all gems in sparkling showers ;
>   In purple was she robed, and of her feast
>   Monarchs partook, and deemed their dignity increased.

XVII.

MODE OF LIFE IN VENICE.

At Venice, Byron shut himself in his chamber, and
nothing was more strange than his mode of life.   He
questions the memories of the past, revives the ruins of
a people who once were what the English now are ;
studies Armenian in the Convent of San Lazaro (1),
prostrates himself before the Helen of Canova (2), visits
the galleries of art, but without indication of due ap-
preciation for the beautiful (3).   " Depend upon it, of all
the arts, it (painting) is the most artificial and unnatural,
and that by which the nonsense of mankind is most im-
posed upon.   I never yet saw the picture or statue which
came a league within my conception, or expectation, but
I have seen many mountains, and seas, and views, and
two or three women who went far beyond it—besides
some horses, and a lion (at Veli Pacha's) in the Morea,
and a tiger at supper in Exeter Change (4)."

(1) Childe Harold, Canto 4.

At the same time he seems to have dictated to himself the Epicurean maxim " eat, drink, and be merry, for to morrow we die." His mother was no more ; a coal mine had been discovered on his estates; large remuneration had been given for the publication of his works (5) so that, no longer straitened in circumstances, he found himself liberally provided with everything suitable to his position. Strange caprice ! He had his horses brought to Venice, and there, on the strand of the Lido, he took his gallop. After passing the entire day in a city where no blade of grass or shrub grows, Byron, nurtured amidst mountains, must needs have the illusive pleasure of again bounding over a verdant soil ; and, in presence of the immensity of the ocean, gallop from the ruined fort as far as the rock he had selected as his tomb, with the epitaph, " *Byron implorat pacem.*" To the rides succeed the gondola, then swimming, and then training his monkeys and dogs, and castigation of the raven for devouring the magpie's food, and pistol shooting. In this exercise he was very skilful, and prided himself on it (1). " I think there are three things I can do which you cannot," he had said to Dr. Polidori, who defied him to name them. " I can swim across that river (2)—I can snuff out that candle with a pistol shot at 20 paces—and I have written a poem of which 14,000 copies were sold in one day." (3) The air of Venice intoxicated him. Scarcely arrived, he falls in love with the wife of a merchant, in whose house he had taken up his abode : then, he abandons the house and love of Marianna (6) to occupy a marble palace on the Grand Canal (4) : he next buys a villa on the banks of the Brenta (5) lovely by nature and art, and worthy of a Doge, and here abandons himself to all the delights of a Southern clime.

There, he has theatricals, the Ridotto, the music of Rossini, and the *bautta rosa*, and the frantic enjoyments of the *Mardi Gras*, inebriating himself with wines and *aguardiente*, surrounded by swaggering and brawling

(1) *Moore's Life*, 1830, p. 104, vol. II.
(2) The Rhine, *Moore's Life*, 1830, p. 30, vol. II.
(3) "The Corsair." *Ibid.*
(4) The Palazzo Mocenigo.
(5) La Mira.

retainers; and, amidst maddening play, and women, and challenges, and rivalries, and all the ribaldry of disorder, Venice believes the carnival and gala days of the past are revived, and follows after this Cavalier. Every one talks of the *young English nobleman with the odd name*, who *lavishes so profuse* an expenditure : every conversazione desires to fête him : every traveller seeks him out : all the women look for a glance from his eye, —a favour, indeed, it was not difficult to obtain. From the high-born dame he passes to the market wench, from the palace to the fisherman's hut. "Venice pleases me as much as I expected, and I expected much. * * * * It is a very good place for women. I like the dialect and their manner very much. There is a *naiveté* about them which is very winning, and the romance of the place is a mighty adjunct; the *bel sangue*, is not, however, now amongst the *dame* or higher orders, but all under *i fazzioli*, or kerchiefs (a white kind of veil which the lower orders wear upon their heads ...the *vesta Zendale*, or old national female costume, is no more. [The city, however, is decaying daily, and does not gain in popula-tion. 6] However, I prefer it to any other in Italy ; and here I pitched my staff, and here I do purpose to reside for the remainder of my life * * &c., &c." (7)

XVIII.

LA FORNARINA.

The most romantic being whom the poet encountered was the Fornarina. He thus speaks of her :

Since you desire the story of Margarita Cogni you shall be told it, though it may be lengthy.

Her face is of the fine Venetian cast of the old time ; her figure, though perhaps too tall, is not less fine—and taken altogether in the national dress.

(6) The Italian author has not thought it needful to repeat the lines within brackets.
(7) *Moore's Life*, 1830, pp. 60 & 167.—Letters to Mr. Murray & Rogers.

D

In the summer of 1817, Hobhouse and myself were sauntering on horse-back along the Brenta one evening, when, amongst a group of peasants, we remarked two girls as the prettiest we had seen for some time. About this period there had been great distress in the country, and I had a little relieved some of the people. Generosity makes a great figure at very little cost in Venetian *lire*, and mine had probably been exaggerated as an Englishman's. Whether they remarked us looking at them or no, I know not; but one of them called out to me, in Venetian, "Why do not you, who relieve others, think of us also?" I turned round and answered her, "Cara, tu sei troppo bella e giovane per aver bisogna del soccorso mio." She answered, "If you saw my hut and my food, you would not say so." All this passed half jestingly, and I saw no more of her for some days.

A few evenings after, we met with these two girls again, and they addressed us more seriously, assuring us of the truth of their statements. They were cousins; Margarita married, the other single. As I doubted still of the circumstances, I took the business in a different light, and made an appointment with them for the next evening. In short, in a few evenings, we arranged our affairs, and for a long space of time she was the only one who preserved over me an ascendancy which was often disputed and never impaired. The reasons of this were—firstly, her person, very dark, tall, the Venetian face, very fine black eyes. She was 22 years old. . . . She was, besides a thorough Venetian in her dialect, in her thoughts, in her countenance, in everything, with all their *naiveté* and pantaloon humour.

Besides, she could neither read nor write, and could not plague me with her letters, except twice that she paid sixpence to a public scribe under the Piazza to make a letter for her, upon some occasion when I was ill, and could not see her. In other respects she was somewhat fierce, and *prepotente*, that is, overbearing, and used to walk in whenever it suited her, with no very great regard to time, place, nor persons, and if she found any women in her place, she knocked them down.

When I first knew her I was in *relazione* (liaison) with La Signora Legati, who was silly enough, one evening at Dolo, accompanied by some of her female friends, to threaten her; for the gossips of the Villeggiatura had already found out, by the neighing of my horse one evening, that I used to ride late in the night to meet the Fornarina. Margarita threw back her veil (*fazziolo*), and replied, in very explicit Venetian, "You are *not* his wife. *I* am *not* his *wife*. You are his *Donna*, and I am his *Donna*. Your husband is a *becco*, and mine is another. For the rest, what *right* have you to reproach me? If he prefers me to you, is it my fault? If you wish to secure him, tie him to your petticoat string. But do not think to speak to me without a reply, because you happen to be richer than I am." Having delivered this pretty piece of eloquence (which I translated as it was related to me by a bystander) she went on her way, leaving a numerous audience, with Madame . . . to ponder at her leisure on the dialogue between them. When I came to Venice for the winter, she followed, and as she found herself out to be a favourite, she came to me pretty often. But she had inordinate self-love, and was not tolerant of other women. At the "Cavalchina," the masqued ball on the last night of the Carnival, where all the world goes, she snatched off the mask of Madame Contarini, a lady noble by birth and decent in conduct, for no other reason but because she was leaning on my arm. You may suppose what a cursed noise this made, but this is only one of her pranks.

At last, she quarrelled with her husband, and one evening ran away to my house. I told her this would not do. She said she would lie in the street, but not go back in him; that he beat her (the gentle tigress!), spent her money, and scandalously neglected her. As it was midnight I let her stay, and next day there was no moving her at all. Her husband came, roaring and crying, and entreating her to come back—not she. He then applied to the police, and they applied to me. I told them and her husband to *take* her. I did not want her; she had come, and I could not fling her out of the window, but they might conduct her through that or the door if they chose it. She went before the Commissary, but was obliged to return with that *becco ettico*, as she called the poor man, who had a pthisic. In a few days she ran away again. After a precious piece of work she fixed herself in my house, really and truly without my consent, but owing to my indolence and not being able to keep my countenance—for if I began in a rage, she always finished by making me laugh with some Venetian buffoonery or another; and the gipsy knew this well enough as well as her other powers of persuasion, and exerted them with the usual tact and success of all she-things—high and low, they are all alike for that.

Madame Benzoni also took her under her protection, and then her head turned. She was always in extremes, either angry or laughing, and so fierce when angered that she was the terror of men, women, and children—for she had the strength of an Amazon, with the temper of Medea. She was a fine animal, but quite untameable. I was the only person that could at all keep her in any order, and when she saw me really angry (which they tell me is a savage sight) she subsided. But she had a thousand fooleries. In her fazziolo, the dress of the lower orders, she looked beautiful; but, alas! she longed for a hat and feathers, and all I could say or do (and I said much) could not prevent this travestie. I put the first into the fire, but I got tired of burning them before she did of buying them, so that she made herself a figure—for they did not at all become her.

Then she would have her gowns with *a tail*—like a lady, forsooth, nothing would serve her but *l'abito colla coua*, or *cua* (that is the Venetian for *la cola*, the tail or train), and as her cursed pronunciation of the word made me laugh, there was an end of all controversy, and she dragged this diabolical tail after her everywhere.

In the meantime, she beat the women and stopped my letters. I found her one day pondering over one. She used to try to find out by their shape whether they were feminine or no, and she used to lament her ignorance, and actually studied her alphabet on purpose (as she declared) to open all letters addressed to me, and read their contents.

I must not omit to do justice to her housekeeping qualities. After she came into my house as " donna di governo " the expenses were reduced to less than half, and everybody did their duty better. The apartments were kept in order, and everything and everybody else, except herself.

That she had a sufficient regard for me in her wild way I had many reasons to believe. I will mention one. In the autumn, one day, going to the Lido with my gondoliers, we were overtaken by a heavy squall and the gondola put in peril—hats blown away, boat filling, oar lost, tumbling sea, thunder, rain in torrents, night coming on, and wind increasing. On our return, after a tight struggle, I found her on the open steps of the Mocenigo Palace, on the Grand Canal, with her great black eyes flashing through her tears, and the long dark hair, which was streaming, drenched with rain, over her brow and breast. She was perfectly exposed to the storm; and the wind blowing her hair and dress about her thin tall figure, and the lightning flashing around her, and the waves rolling at her feet, made her look like Medea alighted from her chariot, or the Sybil of the tempest that was rolling around her—the only living thing within hail at the moment except ourselves. On seeing me safe, she did not wait to greet me, as might have been expected, but calling out to me—"Ah! can' della Madonna, xe esto il tempo per andar al' Lido" (Ah! dog of the Virgin, is this a time to go to Lido)—ran into the house; and solaced herself with scolding the boatmen for not foreseeing the *temporale*. I am told by the servants that she had only been prevented from coming in a boat to look after me by the refusal of all the gondoliers of the canal to put out into the harbour at such a moment, and that then she sate down on the steps, in all the thickest of the squall, and would neither be removed nor comforted. Her joy at seeing me again was moderately mixed with ferocity, and gave me the idea of a tigress over her recovered cubs.

But her reign drew to a close. She became quite ungovernable some months after, and a concurrence of complaints, some true, and many false—"a favourite has no friends"—determined me to part with her. I told her quietly that she must return home (she had acquired a sufficient provision for herself and her mother, &c., in my service), and she refused to quit the house. I was firm, and she threatening knives and revenge. I told her that I had seen knives drawn before her time, and that if she chose to begin there was a knife and fork also at her service on the table, and that intimidation would not do. The next day, while I was at dinner, she walked in (having broken open a glass door that led from the hall below to the staircase by way of prologue), and advancing straight up to the table, snatched the knife from my hand, cutting me slightly in the thumb in the operation. Whether she meant to use this against herself or me I know not—probably against neither—but Fletcher seized her by the arms and disarmed her. I then called my boatmen and desired them to get the gondola ready and conduct her to her own house again, seeing carefully that she did herself no mischief by the way. She seemed quite quiet, and walked downstairs. I resumed my dinner.

We heard a great noise, and went out, and met them on the staircase carrying her upstairs. She had thrown herself into the canal. That she intended to destroy herself, I do not believe; but when we consider the fear women and men, who can't swim, have of deep or even of shallow water (and the Venetians in particular, though they live on the waves), and that it was also night, and dark and very cold, it shows that she had a devilish spirit of some sort within her. They had got her out without much difficulty or damage, excepting the salt water she had swallowed and the wetting she had undergone.

I foresaw her intention to re-fix herself, and sent for a surgeon, enquiring how many hours it would require to restore her from her agitation; and he named the time. I then said, "I give you that time, and more if you require it; but at the expiration of this prescribed period if *she* does not leave the house *I* will." All my people were consternated. They had always been frightened at her, and were now paralysed. They wanted me to apply to the police to guard myself, &c., &c., like a pack of snivelling servile boobies as they were. I did nothing of the kind, thinking that I might as well end that way as another; besides, I had been used to savage women, and I knew their ways.

I had her sent home quietly after her recovery, and never saw her since, except twice at the opera at a distance amongst the audience. She made many attempts to return, but no more violent ones. And this is the story of Margarita Cogni as far as it relates to me.

[I forgot to mention that she was very devout, and would cross herself if she heard the prayer time strike.   .   .   .   .   .

She was quick in reply; as for instance: one day, when she had made me very angry with beating somebody or other, I called her a *cow* (*cow* in Italian, is a sad affront). I called her "Vacca." She turned round,

curtsied, and and answered: "Vacca tua *'celenza*" (i.e., *eccelenza*).
"Your cow, please your excellency." In short, she was, as I said before,
a very fine animal, (1) of considerable beauty and energy, with many
good and several amusing qualities, but wild as a witch and fierce as a
demon. She used to boast publicly of her ascendancy over me, contrasting it with that of other women, and assigning for it sundry reasons.
. . . . . True it was that they all tried to get her away, and no
one succeeded till her own absurdity helped them. (1.)]

I omitted to tell you her answer when I reproached her for snatching
Madame Contarini's mask at the Cavalchina. I represented to her that
she was a lady of high birth, "una dama, &c." She answered "Se ella
è dama *mi (io)* son Veneziana." "If she is a lady, I am a Venetian!"
This would have been fine a hundred years ago. [The pride of the nation
rising up against the pride of aristocracy. But, alas! Venice and her
people and her nobles are alike returning fast to the ocean; and where
there is no independence there can be no real self-respect. (2)]

. . . .

XIX.

MANFRED AND PARISINA, &c.

The poet's noble heart was not, however, formed to
become brutalized in shameless orgies and amidst facile
amours, nor in dissolute banquets :—

> Where revel calls, and laughter, vainly loud,
> False to the heart, distorts the hollow cheek,
> To leave the flagging spirit doubly weak;
> Still o'er the features, which perforce they cheer,
> To feign the pleasure, or conceal the pique;
> Smiles from the channel of a future tear,
> Or raise the writhing lip with ill-dissembled sneer. (1)

He turned then more unto himself, and became again the
great poet. Then was it he completed "Childe Harold's
Pilgrimage," where we may have to censure a disordered,
often an unbridled, imagination; frequent negligence, a
confusion of ideas, vague, incoherent, without connection, and at times obscure. But the impartial reader will
admire the vivid sentiments, and the vigour of thought,
allied to a magic style, which causes one of his most
declared enemies to pronounce the Pilgrimage the most
truly sublime poem ever traced by mortal pen.

(1) The paragraphs within brackets have been omitted by the Italian
author.—Ed.
(2) *Moore's Life*, 1830, pp. 183 to 189.
( ) Childe Harold, Canto 2.

Meantime from every object he derives flashes of imagination. He remarks one day, in the Doges' palace, the empty picture frame of one of them who had been beheaded. (1) That glance suffices, and we have Marino Faliero. Another day Lewis translates him, *vivá voce*, some passages of Goethe's Faust (he was ignorant of the German tongue) ; Manfred follows. But to say truth, the sin of plagiarism (2), with which Goethe charged him in his eulogy of that play, appears scarcely well-founded, since, in fact, Goethe himself has taken both the title and the story of his drama from others. (2) Byron professed to have derived his chief inspiration from the sight of the Swiss Alps. (3) For in Manfred there is no descent into the trivialities of every-day life. Very differently is the subject treated from the mode in which Goethe portrays the being duped by the malice of Mephistopheles.

Byron places his hero in a scene of unsurpassable magnificence, and suited to the mind of Manfred. Goethe brings on the stage the very dregs of the people, and their language is that of the market place and the *cabaret*. The love of Faust is that of a villain ; he destroys the innocence of poor Marguerite, who, on his account, is brought to the scaffold. Alas ! and she,

> In unsurpassing innocence a child
> Hard by that torrent's brink, in tiny cot,
> Upon her little patch and mountain lea,
> With all her homely joys and cares, begot
> And bounded in that little world.
> And I, the abhorr'd of God,—'twas not
> Enough that down with me, I whirl'd
> The rifled rocks and shatter'd them. I must
> Drag her—her and her peace, into the dust !

Byron instead adorned Astarte with every perfection : her shade appears but as a dream, and, passing by, only touhces on the crime of Manfred. The German, with a boldness of thought without parallel, but at the expense of morality and religious sentiment, curses hope, faith, and above all, endurance ; denudes reason and knowledge of their honour ; disdains the supreme energy of man, and would destroy not only all the consolations of the present existence, by showing how man is ever destined from the cradle to misfortune, but even those which in suffer-

---

(2) *Ueber Kunst und Alterthum*, 1820.

ing bring such healing balm by indicating a reward and repose beyond the grave. Byron, on the other hand, tells us of other beings superior to man. The Abbot of St. Maurice directs the mind of Manfred to Heaven, though the heart of the latter was already hardened, and, as he beholds him expiring, he exclaims : " He's gone—his soul hath ta'en its earthless flight—whither, I dread to think—but he is gone."

Faust is a magician alike with Manfred ; his boundless knowledge saves him not from wearisome of life : he " passes, reeling, from lusting to enjoyment, and in enjoyments languishes with desire." To escape, he makes a compact with the evil one, who, in the sequel, will bear him away. With Manfred, the conflict of a noble intelligence with his own thoughts is most terrible ; nor with the new Prometheus does his own strength assist him otherwise than to render him more and more sensible of the sufferings of his punishment. Sole actor is Manfred, his punishment the only action of the drama. No superior power rules him but that of an implacable conscience ; the abuse of the gift of intellect and misguided passions, above all pride, drag him to perdition. And truly is it a sublime lesson, that of a being of boundless wealth, wisdom, and power, and who yet is miserable through remorse.

To this period of the poet's life belongs also Parisina, a poem not of horror, but of which the characteristic is *pity*, a theme less of sensual delight than of sorrow. It is, perhaps, the most powerful of Byron's productions, and that wherein the exquisite sense of the beautiful is most to be admired. (4)

XX.

BEAUTIES OF BYRON'S POEMS.

But, in the portrayal of the beautiful, it seems the ancients, who were in that respect so great, followed altogether a different mode from the poets of modern days. Since they, illumined by a sun for ever unclouded, in a land perpetually smiling, depicted merely the nature before them, without striving to search deeper ; they portrayed it solely for the pleasure of so doing, and regaled us with pictures soft and pleasing to our imagination. The poets of the present day, those especially of the north, either less favoured in clime or because they have come after, feared comparison, sought the more hidden beauty and nature of things, and studied deeply the proofs of these. Less disinterested, therefore, was their portraiture ; nor with rapid conception did they grasp the surface merely, but with exquisite depth of research dived into the more hidden arcana of life. In vain would you seek amongst the ancients for profound knowledge of the heart and analysis of the affections.

Now, Lord Byron, a native of the north, but who for inspiration came to the ardent climes of the South and East, together with a harmony the rarest and most difficult of combination, was supreme in both these faculties, the most certain proof of a boundless intellect. Already, from numerous extracts here and there introduced, we must have manifested how he depicts the scenes of nature so that we actually see them before us ; yet we cannot refrain from giving space to other citations, and first, to the opening lines of the " Bride of Abydos," one of the most truly impassioned of poems. Examples of the beautiful are never superfluous.

> Know ye the land where the cypress and myrtle,
>   Are emblems of deeds that are done in their clime:
> Where the rage of the vulture, the love of the turtle,
>   Now melt into sorrow, now madden to crime?
>
> Know ye the land of the cedar and vine,
> Where the flow'rs ever blossom, the beams ever shine ;
> Where the light wings of zephyr, oppress'd with perfume,
> Wax faint o'er the gardens of Gul in her bloom ;
> Where the citron and olive are fairest of fruit,
> And the voice of the nightingale never is mute ;
> Where the tints of the earth and the hues of the sky
> In colour though varied, in beauty may vie,
> And the purple of ocean is deepest in dye.
> Where the virgins are soft as the roses they twine,
> And all save the spirit of man is divine !
> 'Tis the clime of the East : 'tis the land of the Sun—
> Can he smile on such deeds as his children have done?
> Oh ! wild as the accents of lovers farewell,
> Are the hearts which they bear and the tales which they tell. . &c.

Such the commencement of the " Bride of Abydos,"

and scarcely less beautiful, the death of Selim and
Zulèika having been told, is the conclusion :—

> Within the place of thousand tombs
> That shine beneath, though dark above,
> The sad but living cypress glooms,
>   And withers not, though branch and leaf
>   Are stamp'd with an eternal grief,
>   Like early unrequited love. . . &c.

Would you have a scene of horror ?—read the description of the shipwreck in "Don Juan," Canto 2.

Contrast with such scenes a picture of the heart's
workings, as portrayed in the mien and character of the
"Corsair" :—

> Unlike the heroes of each ancient race,
> Demons in act, but gods at least in face;
> In Conrad's form seems little to admire,
> Though his dark eyebrow shades a glance of fire.
> Robust, but not Herculean—to the sight
> No giant frame sets forth his common height;
> Yet, on the whole, who paused to look again,
> Saw more than marks the crowd of vulgar men.
> They gaze and marvel how—and still confess
> That thus it is, but why, they cannot guess.
> Sunburnt his cheek; his forehead, high and pale,
> The sable curls in wild profusion veil;
> And oft perforce his rising lip reveals
> The haughtier thought it curbs, but scarce conceals. . . &c.

Such extracts, however lengthy, are not wearisome,
and they are produced because many have maintained that the author therein would depict himself.
Now, let us observe how "Manfred" reveals the recesses
of his soul to the Destiny of the Alps :—

> Well, though it torture me, 'tis but the same;
> My pangs shall find a voice. From my youth upwards
> My spirit walked not with the souls of men,
> Nor look'd upon the earth with human eyes.
> The thirst of their ambition was not mine;
> The aim of their existence was not mine.
> My joys, my grief, my passions, and my powers
> Made me a stranger; though I wore the form,
> I had no sympathy with breathing flesh;
> Nor, midst the creatures of clay that girded me,
> Was there but one who—but of her anon.
> I said with men, and with the thoughts of men
> I held but slight communion; but instead,
> My joy was in the wilderness to breathe
> The difficult air of the iced mountain's top,
> Where the birds dare not build, nor insect's wing
> Flit o'er the herbless granite; or to plunge
> Into the torrent, and to roll along
> On the swift whirl of the new breaking wave
> Of river, stream, or ocean, in their flow. . . &c.

XXI.

BEPPO AND PARISINA, &c.

But here terminates Lord Byron's first style. Strange as may, however, appear to some the conception of the preceding poems, there yet abound in them splendour and vigour, lamentation the most solemn, and ideas of faith the most consoling. The poet displays himself the sceptic, we allow, but not to the extent of a cold contempt, and amid the eloquence of grief is manifested a desire for immortality. You might liken him to an angel, banish'd from heaven, but still mindful of his celestial origin :—

I look upon the peopled desert past (1)
 As on a place of agony and strife,
Where, for some sin, to sorrow I was cast,
 To act and suffer, but re-mount at last.
With a fresh pinion, which I feel to spring,
 Though young, yet waxing vigorous as the blast
Which it would cope with, on delighted wing,
Spurning the clay cold bonds which round our being cling.

 Are not the mountains, waves, and skies a part
  Of me and of my soul, as I of them ?
 Is not the love of these deep in my heart
  With a pure passion ?.
         . &c.

But now, to a vivid, inspired, free poesy, colored with memories and by hope, from which breathes forth a freshness of feeling as yet untarnished by the bitter blast of experience, succeeds one inspired by animosity and pitiless sarcasm, which delights in denuding virtue itself of its charm, which covers itself with the mask of Aristophanes to mock with angry derision at all, whether Socrates or Sophist.

Beppo, a Venetian tale, wherein he depicts *cicisbeism*, first betrays this tendency to aberration. In "Don Juan," he plunges headlong into the offending vortex.

That "Don Juan," whom we have all seen on the public stage hurried away by the demon before his time, the Spanish Don Juan (2), in whom Moliere found the only type of contrast for his Tartuffe, and whom Mozart

(1) Childe Harold, Canto 3.
(2) De Stendhahl. See Appendix.

re-embellished with the harmonious strains of a glorious music,—this character would Byron revive. Nor is he now that effeminate libertine and triumphant egotist who would create vice into a system and make a display of it, as vulgar tradition has given us to suppose.

Byron's hero indulges in his amours in the series; allowing himself to be borne along on the torrent of his pleasures or of opinion; nothing unsavoury deters him; he analyses not too closely; for the rest, he is brave and daunted by no peril. but on occasions can doubt or blaspheme, as if he had studied Diderot (1) and his school. In the main, this character is not so well-drawn or sustained throughout as the others Byron has portrayed; and we may easily believe Mr. Hunt that the poet himself would write off his stanzas without very well knowing how they would end (3). In fact, after the Third Canto, he drags his hero into most startling adventures, and Byron is not great when he depicts adventure, but rather when he analyses man, when his world is the human heart. But, good God! under what aspect does the noble lord set himself to contemplate human nature!

It is no longer the recluse of Geneva, who sadly regards the vices of society, with the desire of probing its wounds and then curing them; you encounter rather the philosopher of Ferney (from whose delineations this poem might seem suggested), who opposes sensibility and ridicules noble actions by showing their secret motives —a philosophy which will not lead to crime, but which tends to wither the highest virtues and all social charity, to destroy, moreover, respect for the human species, which, whether founded on illusions or not, we trust to heaven we (and those around us) shall never lose, so deplorable would be the result of the disenchantment.

The idol of love before which he had burned incense, he here despoils of every adornment; here, with cold irony, he scorns all enthusiasm, respecting not even patriotism, nor liberty, nor valour; all is illusion, all vanity, all folly; he laughs at all, but with the laughter of a man crowned with roses, under which the thorns transfix him; he laughs like one who would thus spare himself the bitterness of execration. A doctrine, in fact, so to speak, which,

(3) As is often the case with authors. See *Life of Charles Lever*, &c.—Ed.

should a cynic come to preach it to you in its naked deformity, would cause you only a shudder and nothing more; but which becomes dangerous, identified as it is with a person who likewise attracts our regard, who displays himself to us with all the most noble and consoling illusions, but divests himself of them a moment afterwards to turn them into ridicule, who pays, in fact, court to virtue only to say it is but falsehood, or excites good and generous sentiments but to declare them rediculous and vain (2). No! it is not possible to make war on enthusiasm in a more cruel mode, than with such an admixture of gravity and buffoonery.

> Silent and pensive, idle, restless, slow (4),
>   His home deserted for the lonely wood,
> Tormented with a wound he could not know
>   His, like all deep grief, plunged in solitude;
> I'm fond myself of solitude or so,
>   But then I beg it may be understood,
>   By solitude I mean a Sultan's, not
>   A hermit's, with a harem for a grot. . . &c.

On Greece, revived again, he pours forth a lay abounding in the noblest of sentiments—but how? He places it in the mouth of a poet at a banquet—who sings for every faction, who flatters all in power, who knows not either vice or virtue if it be not self-interest (3).

Do you remember how in his " Pilgrimage " he depicted the Castilian maids when speaking of the war which, with their countrymen, they waged against the French invader?

> Is it for this the Spanish maid, aroused (5),
>   Hangs on the willow her unstrung guitar,
> And, all unsex'd, the anlace hath espous'd,
>   Sung the loud song, and dared the deed of war,
>   And she, whom once the semblance of a scar
> Appalled, an owlet's larum chilled with dread,
> Now views the column scattering, bay'net jar,
>   The falchion flash, and o'er the yet warm dead
>   Stalks with Minerva's step where Mars might quake to tread.
> Ye who shall marvel when you hear her tale,
>   Oh! had you known her in her softer hour,
> Mark'd her black eye that mocks her coal-black veil,
>   Heard her light lively tones in lady's bower,
>   Seen her long locks that foil the painter's power,
> Her fairy form, with more than female grace,
>   Scarce would you deem that Saragoza's tower
> Beheld her smile in danger's Gorgon face
> Thin the closed ranks, and lead in glory's fearful chase (4).

(4) Don Juan, Canto 1.
(5) Don Juan, Canto 3, Stanza 86.

Now, mark how he depicts her in " Don Juan."

> And such sweet girls—I mean such graceful ladies,
> Their very walk would make your bosom swell ;
> I can't describe it, though so much it strike,
> Nor liken it—I never saw the like.

> An Arab horse, a stately stag, a barb
> New broke, a cameleopard, a gazelle,
> No—none of these will do—and then their garb !
> Their veil and petticoat—Alas ! to dwell
> Upon such things would very near absorb
> A Canto—then their feet and ancles —well
> Thank Heaven I've got no metaphor quite ready,
> And so, my sober muse—come, let's be steady—
> &c.

You will willingly spare me, kind reader, the further contrasting of ideas that may be too sacred. After the first two cantos, the intercourse with Italians, who recalled him to the reality of life and greater tranquillity of mind, tempered not a little his bitterness. In the succeeding cantos he conducts Don Juan through the luxurious and thoroughly sensual existence of the harems of the East, then to the Court of Catherine the Second of Russia, thence to England, to form acquaintance with its exclusive society, to deride its prejudices, to lead a life of dissipation in the Abbey at Newstead. Thus were filled up the sixteen Cantos of his poem (5). And it is said he intended to have added more, conducting his hero through the great crimes and great virtues of the French Revolution (6).

This singular poem, which has beauties and defects quite peculiar to itself, where poetry makes trial of every chord, with endless variety of intonation, with an ever wondrous and original expression, with verse easy and spontaneous and also harmonious, with the finest perception varied to infinity in its most minute gradations, was in his own land pitilessly persecuted. Not so much, I believe, for the weapons with which he assailed virtue, as for the lasting injury he gives, and ever will give, to the moral, religious, political, and poetical cant of his country (7). And this, with power greater than would be believed in a land we are accustomed to call *par excellence* free, loaded the author with the purchased abuse of the Reviews, and combined to place Don Juan beyond the pale of protection—that is to say, to endanger the publisher, who, notwithstanding, did his best to circulate the work by numerous editions and at a low price (8).

To a young man, I would recommend Childe Harold; but, alas! let him not approach the frigid anatomy of Don Juan; it cannot, moreover, be in unison with the feelings of young hearts, which, following virtue by instinct rather than calculation, have fortunately not acquired, as yet, the sad discrimination which sees the secret end of every action. An Italian lady one day made some observations to Lord Byron on this poem, and he agreed with her, but replied that he suspected it would live longer than Childe Harold. "Ah, but," said she, "I would rather have the fame of Childe Harold for three years, than an immortality of Don Juan." (6).

XXII.

BYRON'S DRAMAS.

Many other compositions were completed by the poet about this time. The Rev. Mr. Bowles, a Protestant clergyman, in reprinting the works of Pope, had taxed the latter with immorality by the publication of some of his *inedited* letters, and laid down as a canon law of poetry that "all the imagery drawn from that which is beautiful and sublime in any work of nature, is more beautiful and sublime than are the images drawn from art, and in consequence more poetical" (1). By which rule judging Pope, he found in his poetry more of art than nature. Here ensued a contest betwixt himself and Campbell, betwixt the classic and the romantic school, in which Byron interposed his voice. And first, he defends Pope from the stigma of immorality, because of the justice of judging of a man in accordance with the

(6) Letter to Murray, p. 354. *Moore's Life*, vol. 2, p. 1830.

tenor of his life, and not from some isolated fact. Pass
ing thence to literary doctrine, he goes on to say that
the painter and the poet ought not to observe things too
minutely, but through the medium of the sensations they
awaken; that the existence of man or of the arts increases
the poetry of the world's wonders; in fine, he rails
against the herd of poetasters who erected a mosque
by the side of a noble Greek temple, and as he is
ashamed to figure among the constructors of this Tower
of Babel, though certainly he has given no help towards
demolishing the ancient structure, he continues his
diatribe in violent language, which proves how much
man's reason may be perverted if, from love of sophistry,
he combats that which has been the opinion of his whole
life, the essence of all his compositions.

But, so that these new operations should not be without the support of examples, he composed tragedies with
all the unities. He, Byron, in the language of Shakspere, composes tragedies according to the rules of Aristotle. You might liken him to one of those skilful
dancers, who, enveloped in, or rather suspended on
cords, &c., thus test their expertness in *tours de force*, or
fearful leaps. In all his dramas the dialogues and
speeches are too frequent ; every action, every sentiment,
is produced by external means. The heart is there
analysed and depicted in words, instead of being, as is
nearly always the case in Shakspere, revealed by a sign,
a word, or silence. We have too many *embroglios* or
counterplots ; too little of real life is there. In his plays
sway not those passions with power to transport the
audience beyond themselves ; to centre their feelings in
the sufferings and their causes before them.

Marino Faliero, a Doge of Venice, outraged in the
honour of his wife, refused justice by the Council of Ten,
conspires to destroy the Republic, and his plot being discovered, is beheaded on the Giants' Stairs, predicting, as
he dies, the degradation of Venice. (2) Although the
magnanimous sentiments with which the play abounds
cannot but please, this drama is cold and labored, and
the characters, if we except the dignified tenderness of
Angiolina, and the vigorous action of the conspirator,
Bertuccio, are insipid ; there is too little action ; too
many dialogues ; too much of art.

In the "Two Foscari," Jacopo, the son of the Doge
Foscari, from his exile writes to the Duke of Milan,
invoking his aid against his own country. The letter is
intercepted; as a state criminal, he is summoned to
Venice; he hastens to return, confessing to have acted
thus, designedly, with the hope of again beholding his
birthplace and beloved parents. But a powerful enemy
pursues him. Loredano, who, believing the Foscari
guilty of having poisoned his *kinsmen,* has inscribed on
the list of his debtors the Doge *"for the death of my
father and uncle,"* and has done thus much that he might
afterwards note against it: *"he has paid me"* (3). In
fact, at his instigation, Jacopo is again condemned to
exile, but such anguish seizes him at again abandoning
his country that his heart breaks; then the Doge, full
of years and virtues, is deposed from his throne, and
also dies. The patriotic love of Jacopo, the affection of
Marina his wife, the premeditated vengeance of Loredano,
the restrained anguish of the Doge, embellish here and
there this drama, in which, however, the action proceeds
too slowly (1).

In "Sardanapalus" we find not the effeminate Assyrian.
He is a man passionately devoted to the enjoyment of
sensual pleasures, it is true, -but, does danger approach,
his equanimity is disturbed not—he feels no fear.
He is capable of virtue. In place of saying to his subjects,
"Bring me gold, soldiers, the sacrifice of your blood;
worship, adore me, and labour for me;" or of dragging
them where it might then be written: *"Here Sardanapalus
slaughtered 50,000 of his enemies—behold their graves and
his trophies,"* (4) he allows them instead to live in such
tranquillity that they become tired of contentment and
favor an ambitious rival, who drives him from the throne
to the funeral pile. This Sardanapalus is so noble that
his character begets as it were a weariness or monotony.
The dramatic interest is scanty; the priests and warriors
are placed in an obscure light; here and there some
superlatively beautiful passages recompense us (2).

But from self-imposed trammels Byron soon freed
himself in "Werner (5), or the Inheritance," a romance

in dialogue, where the characters are copied from some previously delineated. The plot is taken from a tale by Miss Lee.

In the " Deformed Transformed," Arnoldo, crippled from his birth, is transformed by the Evil One into a young and handsome Cæsar Borgia, and led to witness the sacking of Rome by the soldiers of Charles V. The Demon, accompanying his *protégé*, employs himself in the discouraging task of revealing to him the secret springs of human action ; the vice concealed under the guise of virtue [3].

Everyone can doubtless call to mind the " Mysteries," those representations of sacred events, which, in the Middle Ages, attracted the multitude, and excited its devotion as also its disorders, and which were the first steps toward the revival of the dramatic art. From these it was that Byron actually took the title of two Mysteries, " Cain " and " Heaven and Earth."

XXIII.

BYRON'S OTHER WORKS.

This last depicts to us the eve of the Deluge, and how all men were terror-stricken thereat, except two daughters of Cain, beloved of two angels, who, according to the Hebrew traditions, [1] for them descended to earth. Amid the exultation of the evil spirits, the lamentations of mortals, and the desolation of nature, arrived the fatal hour. Raphael summons back the two angels, but they prefer the loss of beatitude rather than forsake mortal delights, and with these they transpose themselves into other spheres, whilst the waters submerge the world.

The " Cain " might be defined the doctrine, in dialogue, of the origin of evil. Therein, the poet describes the growth of society, and the first-born of man,

[3] The story is founded partly on that of a novel, "The Three Brothers," and partly on the "Faust" of Goethe.
[1] Genesis, chap. 6.   E

tormented by the insatiable thirst of knowledge, by fear of death and life ; human only, in fact, because he loves most affectionately his wife and sister Adah ; and, for the rest, possessed by an overwhelming pride, which causes him to murmur against the Deity and his parents. With his blasphemy accords that of Lucifer, who would persuade him to adore him, and who guides him beyond the limits of the world to contemplate the souls of those who inhabited the earth before Adam (1) until he leads him back to earth, persuaded that the highest wisdom is the knowledge of the nullity of human nature and pre-disposed for the first time, which stained the earth with blood.   This work was deemed scandalous ; outcries were raised at the impiety uttered by the two rebels against the Divine goodness and providence, to which none replied.   The author was styled either Manichean or Atheist, nor was deemed valid the excuse he adduced of having been right in making the actors of his drama speak according to their nature ; or because the Satan of Milton was allowed to affirm that evil is good. (2)

In the "Island," the poet transports Christian far from the evils of civilisation, into the midst of the verdant isles of the Pacific, as yet uncontaminated by arts and the crimes of man, and to an existence where the thoughts are developed but for love only, where man, amid the gifts which are poured upon him by an invisible hand, lives a life of prolonged youth.

Everyone has been horrified at the unheard-of punishments of "Mazeppa," who, bound to a furious horse, goes for many days (how wonderful, how inimitable is the harmony and variety of the verse !) (3) tearing along over deserts and through forests until the steed falls lifeless, and the agonised rider is then saved to become Hetman of the Ukraine, and to relate his dire mishap to Charles XII after his defeat at Pultowa.

The "Vision of Dante" is a lament over Italy.   In the Lament of Tasso we see not exaggerated and fanciful ideas but a solemn restrained grief ; the real minstrel of Godfrey, who consoles himself for a past of love in a future of fame.

Worthy of Dante and Michael Angelo is the conception of "Darkness," wherein is imaged the earth at the moment the sun is extinguished; a calamity so immeasurable that it is painful to contemplate it even through the medium of the most dazzling poetry.

Oftentimes he infuses into lyrics the impressions which either his own misfortunes or the stupendous events agitating the world produced in his mind. In the "Age of Bronze" (²) he bitterly inveighs against the Continental Powers, stripping off the laurels of Europe, and rending the purple of its rulers, to reveal the naked deformity beneath. To Napoleon, with whom he has often been compared (4), he burned not incense in the days of his glory; but when he fell, he reproached him with the vices of his reign (3); when he died, he forgot his ambition, and deplored him, as one consecrated by the majesty of misfortune.

The opening stanzas of the Napoleon Ode, if so we may style it, are of great force.

> Yes! where is he, the Champion and the Child
> Of all that's great or little, wise or mild,
> Whose game was empires, and whose stakes were thrones;
> Whose table earth—whose dice were human bones. . . &c.

We intend not—too long the tale would be—to follow closely and singly all the author's minor works. He contributed to a journal (4), *The Liberal* (5), in the first number of which he inserted the "Vision of Judgment," turning into ridicule the Apotheosis of King George III., composed by Southey; a satirical caricature unworthy of the greatness of one, who, with giant's steps, should have pursued his way, without caring for the petty disturbances raised by the envious pigmies at his feet. But Byron was in this far beneath himself. He ought to have imitated his countryman Pope, who, sorely vexed at a most bitter critique, allowed himself to be persuaded by Addison to answer no otherwise than by a

(²) "The Age of Bronze," or Carmen Seculare et annus haud "mirabilis," 1821.

(3) The "Ode to Napoleon" :—
> 'Tis done! but yesterday a king,
> And now thou art a nameless thing,
> So abject, yet alive, &c.

(4) The *Liberal* (see note at end of Vol.), which lasted only to the fourth number.

fresh composition, and he published the "Essay on
Man." But the periodical insults which the English and
even Italian journals, with dauntless fatuity, launched
incessantly against him upon whom they waged war
as against a proscribed school, disturbed the equanimity
of Byron, who would contend against them, and honour
with his indignant replies these miserable scribblers.
A bitter literary conflict he waged with Southey, the
Poet Laureate, who boasted of having with his sling
smitten on the brow the Goliath whom he denounced
as the head of a *Satanic school*, subversive of political
and moral order. Byron, in fact, was once on the point
of starting from Italy to return to England, for no other
purpose than to call to a deadly account that avowed
champion of the aristocracy ; but a friend induced him
to reflect that the English nobility would have purchased
all the poets to enjoy the satisfaction of having disturbed
the tranquillity of the author of Don Juan.

But, to compose works thus diversified, or even merely
to finish "Don Juan," where so great is the variety, so
versatile the power, of creative genius, that with difficulty
we believe it the work of one hand, was required, (it
would seem) precisely an existence of that character
which Byron led, betwixt annoyances, caprices, dissipation and antipathies, trivial vices and sublime virtues,
elevated sentiments and shameless inclinations. Now the
misanthrope, and now agreeable and gallant; now a despot,
now affable and kind ; here the seducer, there the pro-
tector of innocence and misfortune ; now the egotist and
the miser, then disinterested and generous; now credulous
as a cavalier of the Middle Ages, and then sceptical as
an Encyclopœdist ; to-day he blusters and defies like a
swaggerer and a bully, to-morrow he is the peacemaker
betwixt opponents. On one occasion the desperate
gambler, on another the patient explorer of antiquities ;
from the crowded Ridotto he passes to the study of
Armenian with the monks (1) ; from carousals and dissipation he retires to his study to meditate on the vain
illusions of youth, on dreams of domestic felicity, a country,
a political existence, friends, his daughter, a life he had
already exhausted, when ye but thirty years of age.

(1) In the Armenian Convent.

XXIV.

THE GUICCIOLI.

To divert his mind from this fatiguing inaction, from anticipations of death, what did he still desire? His ever cherished idols, love and liberty. To better habits and another mode of life he in fact returned when he became acquainted with Signora Gamba Guiccioli. Unfortunately, neither with him nor her could a love passion escape without reproach. And truly then might the poet have repeated in his own lines :—

> O God! that we had met in time,
>   Our hearts as fond, thy hand more free;
> When thou hadst loved without a crime
>   And I been less unworthy thee? (1)

Would ye that I should describe to you the merits of Countess Guiccoli? Is it not enough to say that she could enchain an irreclaimable being, and one long disused to seek another heart, another mind, a sympathizing language —one too, who was the author of " Don Juan?" She was scarcely eighteen years of age, and had shortly before left a convent to espouse Count Guiccioli.

"I became acquainted," (2) says Madame Guiccioli, "with Lord Byron in April, 1819; he was introduced to me at Venice by the Countess Benzoni at one of that lady's parties. This introduction, which had so much influence on the lives of us both, took place contrary to our wishes, and had been permitted by us only from courtesy. For myself, more fatigued than usual on account of the late hours they keep in Venice, I went with great reluctance to this party, and purely in obedience to Count Guiccioli. Lord Byron, who was averse to forming new acquaintances,— alleging that he had entirely renounced all attachments and was unwilling any more to expose himself to their consequences—on being requested by the Countess Benzoni to allow himself to be presented to me, refused, and at last only assented from a desire to oblige her. His noble and ex-

(1) " Remember him, whom passion's power."—*Occasional Pieces.*

(2) *Moore's Life*, &c.—Byron had, however, seen the Countess Teresa Gamba at Countess Albrizzi's, in 1818, just after her nuptials.—ED.

quisitely beautiful countenance, the tone of his voice, his manners, the thousand enchantments that surrounded him, rendered him so different and so superior a being to any whom I had hitherto seen, that it was impossible he should not have left the most profound impression upon me. From that evening, during the whole of my subsequent stay in Venice, we met every day, &c." It boots not to relate here the story of their loves, nor need we repeat any of his letters to her—they are, according to custom, variations only, of the perpetual theme, " *ti amo.*"

Scandal resulted from the connection; for, as Byron had been obliged to forsake his wife—a cold and passionless lady —so the Guiccioli was to separate from her aged husband; and the poet and this lady clung only the closer in their affection for each other. He abandoned Venice to follow her to Bologna, to Ravenna. At Ravenna the lady was brought by illness to the point of death : the presence of Byron restored her to life. And here the fear of losing her, the satisfaction of beholding her recovery, gratitude, reciprocal attentions, walks in each other's company—if ever Byron had a moment's contentment, it was here. His thoughts full of her, he now visited the tomb of Gaston de Foix; now that of Dante; or he wandered pensive through the pine forests on the Chiassi, and tuned his lyre to responses of unwonted sounds of plaintive sweetness.

> Ave Maria ! o'er the earth and sea,
>   That heavenliest hour of Heaven is worthiest thee !
> Ave Maria ! blessed be the hour,
>   The time, the clime, the spot, where I so oft
> Have felt that moment in its fullest power,
>   Sink o'er the earth so beautiful and soft ;
> While swung the deep bell in the distant tower,
>   Or the faint dying day-hymn stole aloft,
>   And not a breath crept through the rosy air,
>   And yet the forest leaves seemed stirr'd with prayer. &c.

One would say that these are the impassioned verses of Childe Harold, not of the scornful and sceptical Don Juan. But " Don Juan," that poem of which the exhortations of all his friends had not induced him to change a single line, remained uncompleted. Could the perpetual sarcasm, wherewith it pleased him to denude woman of every illusion, be now befitting him, when he acknowledged the empire of one? Or, could that hysterical mockery of laughter, so akin to grief, be now

the greeting for one then so favored? Henceforth, the
entreaties of the lady stopped his pen, (1) nor did he
resume the poem till long afterwards, and then, as is
clearly apparent, he changed its tenor.

One day (it was at Bologna, the 24th of August, 1819),
he found his mistress absent from the house. Alone,
pensive, he wanders through her apartments, thus·
reviving all his cherished recollections; then he pauses
to seat himself beside a fountain, and meditates and
weeps. There, where often they had been seated
together side by side, he finds the "Corinne" of Madame
de Stael, left on this spot by her he loves, and thus he
writes upon its leaves :—

My dearest Theresa,—I have read this book in your garden—my
love, you were absent, or else I could not have read it. It is a favorite
book of yours, and the writer was a friend of mine. You will not understand these English words, others will not understand them—which is the
reason I have not scrawled them in Italian. But you will recognise the
handwriting of him who passionately loved you, and you will divine that
over a book, which was yours, he could only think of love. In that
word, beautiful in all languages, but most so in yours—*amor mio*—is
composed my existence here and hereafter (4) [I feel I exist here, and I
fear that I shall exist hereafter—to what purpose you will decide; my
destiny rests with you, and you are a woman, 18 years of age, and two
out of a convent. I wish you had *staid* there with all my heart—or at
least that I had never met you in your married state. But all this is
too late.] I love you and you love me—at least you say so, and act as
if you did so, which last is a great consolation in all events. But I more
than love you, and cannot cease to love you. Think of me sometimes
when the Alps and Ocean divide us—they never will, unless you·
wish it.

BYRON (5).

Bologna, August 25, 1819.

To the splendid English edition of Lord Byron's
works is attached the portrait of the Guiccioli. Lady
Byron, solicited to give her picture also, refused to
appear thus in a work along with the Italian lady. The
editors then maliciously displayed to her a frightful portrait, saying that, since they were obliged to keep faith·
with the public, they would insert that as her picture.
The lady, to avoid appearing thus to disadvantage in a
work wherein the beauty of Guiccioli was so con-·
spicuously displayed, allowed herself to be persuaded to·
have her picture taken again.

Without wishing to test the truth of this anecdote, we·

(4) The paragraphs in brackets are omitted by the author, Cantù.
(5) *Moore's Life.*

think Lady Byron's scruples proper and natural. (6)   We
give below a sketch of both ladies :—

There was something piquant, and what we term pretty, in Miss Millbank; her features were small and feminine, though not regular. She
had the finest skin imaginable; her figure was perfect for her height;
and there was a simplicity, a retired modesty, about her which was very
characteristic, and formed a happy contrast to the cold and artificial
formality and studied stiffness which is called fashion. She interested
me exceedingly, &c.—*Lord Byron's own Conversations.*

The Countess Guiccioli is 23 years of age, though she appears no more
than 17 or 18. Unlike most of the Italian women, her complexion is
delicately fair. Her eyes, large, dark, and languishing, are shaded by
the longest eyelashes in the world; and her hair, which is ungathered
on her head, plays over her falling shoulders in a profusion of natural
ringlets of the darkest auburn. Her figure is perhaps too much embonpoint for her height; but her bust is perfect. Her features want little
of possessing a Grecian regularity of outline; and she has the most
beautiful mouth and teeth imaginable. It is impossible to see without
admiring—to hear the Guiccioli speak without being fascinated, &c.
. . . . . .—Extracts from *Life by Bulwer.*

XXV.

HIS MEMOIRS.

And yet of this man such evil rumours spread as of
one both brutal and ferocious.   That puerile curiosity
which attaches to the steps of the great sought out
every minute circumstance of his life, and he was displayed without mask to the world, just, we may say,
as so many things which he has himself denuded, and
over which a veil had been better cast.   Certainly,
from the delineations of so many friends and enemies, the
multitude of which might almost form a library, the poet
gained nothing : so much so, that none could distinguish
what was real in him from that which was but the bold
and ostentatious assumption of vice and cynicism.   But
the entire revelation of his real mind, the display of the
source of his virtues, the excuse for his vices (since often
that which appears crime is but misfortune), could be
only the work of Byron himself.   For this cause he
dreaded biographies, and when La Theotochi Albrizzi (1)
at Venice made known to him that she had sketched

(6) Editor.
(1) A native of Corfu, styled by Byron " The Venetian De Stael."

him in one of her portraits (" Ritratti ") he refused to
see it and begged her to destroy it.   To Lady Blessington, however, he confessed to have been twice under
obligation to such friends, since they had preserved him
from suicide. (2)   " It is a fact," said he, seeing me look
grave, " I assure you I should positively have destroyed
myself, but I guessed that —— would write my life, and
with this fear before my eyes, I have lived on.   I know
so well the sort of things they would write of me—the
excuses, lame as myself, that they would offer for my
delinquencies while they were unnecessarily exposing
them, and all this done with the avowed intention of
justifying what, God help me ! cannot be justified, my
unpoetical reputation, with which the world can have
nothing to do ! One of my friends would dip his pen in
clarified honey, and the other in vinegar, to describe my
manifold transgressions, and as I do not wish my poor
fame to be either *preserved* or *pickled*, I have lived on and
written my memoirs, where facts will speak for themselves without the editorial candour of excuses such as
' we cannot excuse *this* unhappy error, or defend *that*
impropriety,'—the mode in which friends exalt their own
prudence and virtue, by exhibiting the want of those
qualities in the dear departed, and by marking their
disapproval of his errors.   I have written my memoirs,"
said Byron, " to save the necessity of their being written
by a friend, or friends, and have only to hope they will
not add notes."

Thomas Moore, the poet, who has depicted the East,
whom Byron honored more than most persons with his
friendship, was dining one day at Venice, in the latter's
house.   Before the repast is over, his Lordship leaves the
room and returns laden with an enormous bundle of
papers (in a white leather bag.) (1)   " Look here," he
said, holding it up, " this would be something to make
John Murray (his publisher) laugh."   " What papers are
those ? " demanded the Anacreon.   " Nothing less than
my memoirs," replied Byron.   " I give them to you, let who
will read them, but they ought not to be published while
I am alive." (3)   And Moore received the sacred deposit.

(2) *Conversations of Lady Blessington with Lord Byron*, p. 57.

(3) It was decided that they were not suitable for publication.

Afterwards, Byron wrote to Murray more than once.. " Buy my memoirs of Moore, buy them at a good price ; since, in the first place, he wants money, and next, they will repay you well. I have not very long to live." (4)

Conceive the importance of these papers. To men of let- ters the exquisite delight of a new prose work by Byron ; for the biographer, the men and occurrences of the day and contemporary literature; for the philosopher, the analysis of the human heart, a narration resembling the Confessions of Jean Jacques, or the Life of Alfieri, in resemblance to whom he had been exiled from his native home, wandered from land to land, maintained a stud of horses, (2) loved another man's wife, and deplored fair Italy. Those memoirs are in the hands of a friend. So that, when Europe had to lament the untimely loss of the poet, it yet found a kind of consolation in the knowledge that he would then re-appear to the world as depicted by himself. But what? Moore, the friend, the confidant, the inheritor of Byron, betrays his friend, his country, the world. For we know not what trivial reasons, in deference to Lady Byron, possibly on account of a consideration received from a certain set to whom they might cause umbrage, he burns these memoirs. No ! he who does not feel himself capable of preserving as he ought the heritage of a great man,· renounces it, or should draw upon himself opprobrium and execration. But, as from the publication of so important a work Moore must have looked for large profits, doubt not that he knew how to consummate the treason without throwing away the thirty pieces. For six thousand pounds he stipulates with the bookseller—and behold in five volumes appear the " Memoirs of Byron." The greedy public rushes to obtain them : it is but a perpetual commentary of this same Irish Anacreon. But the numerous letters, altho' the facts be there mutilated and the names suppressed— the few fragments of Byron's Journal, as they still are much for him who would again restore that monument with the zeal and good faith which Moore lacked— render still more ardent the desire for the original papers where Byron, Byron himself, was his own

(4) Moore received two thousand pounds or guineas from Mr. Murray for the MS. See Anon.

biographer, and which are irreparably lost. We know
not if the name of Moore as a poet will descend to far
posterity, nor care we ; but if so, it should be in company
with that Erostratus who obtained an infamous notoriety
by burning the most celebrated temple of Greece. (3)

The world has probably been satisfied with the
compilation by Moore of Lord Byron's · letters and
journals, if not with his biography of the poet. The
editor here, however, gives, from Sir H. L. Bulwer's Life
of Byron, an extract touching Mr. Moore's conduct with
regard to the memoirs. " Several years ago, Lord Byron
presented his friend, Mr. Thos. Moore, with his memoirs,
written by himself, with an understanding that they were
not to be published until after his death. Mr. Moore,
with the consent and at the desire of Lord Byron, sold
the MS. to Mr. Murray, the bookseller, for the sum of two
thousand guineas. The following statement by Mr. Moore,
will, however, show its fate :—' Without entering into
the respective claims of Mr. Murray and myself to the
property in these memoirs (a question which, now that
they are destroyed, can be but of little moment to any
one), it is sufficient to say, that, believing the MS. still
to be mine, I placed it at the disposal of Lord Byron's
sister, Mrs. Leigh, with the sole reservation of a protest
against its total destruction ; at least, without previous
perusal and consultation among the parties. The
majority of the persons present disagreed with this
opinion, and it was the *only point* upon which there did
exist any difference between us. The MS. was accordingly
torn and burnt before our eyes, and I immediately paid
to Mr. Murray, in the presence of gentlemen assembled,
the two thousand guineas, with interest, &c., being the
amount of what I owed him upon the security of Mr. Bond,
and for which I now stand indebted to my publishers,
Messrs. Longman and Co. Since then, the family of
Lord Byron have, in a manner highly honorable to
themselves, proposed an arrangement by which the sum
thus paid to Mr, Murray might be reimbursed to me ;
but from feelings and considerations which it is
unnecessary here to explain, I have respectfully but
peremptorily, declined their offer.''' (⁵)

(5) Johnson's Lives of the Poets, continued by Hazlitt.

XXVI.

THE ITALIANS AND FAME.

But our business is with the poet himself, who, from Venice, where he had believed his home was fixed, became compelled, either by affection or from motives of security, to wander to various parts of Italy.

He was long at Ravènna, then at Pisa, where he inhabited the Lanfranchi Palace, formerly the residence of the ancient persecutor of Ugolino; from thence, through a quarrel with a military officer, he was obliged to change his abode to Genoa, having thus occasion to observe various portions of our beautiful land. Indeed, he vaunted his thorough knowledge of it, but we must not believe him, nor would our readers, if they would give attention to the prejudiced opinions be pronounced upon it. Here, in addition to those that precede it, are some amongst them :—

To Mr. Murray.

Ravenna, 1st February, 1820.

.   .   .   .   .   .   Their moral is not your moral ; their life is not your life; you would not understand it [it is not English, nor French, nor German]. The conventual education, the *cavalieri servienti*, the habits of thought and living, are so entirely different, and the difference becomes so much the more striking the more you live intimately with them, that I know not how to make you comprehend a people who are at once temperate and profligate, serious in their characters and buffoons in their amusements, capable of impressions and passions which are at once hidden and durable (what we could call so), as you may see by their comedies; they have no real comedy, not even in Goldoni, and that is because they have no society to draw it from.

Their *conversazioni* are not society at all. They go to the theatre to talk, and into company to hold their tongues. The *women* sit in a circle, and the men gather into groups, or they play at dreary *faro* or *lotto reale* for small sums. Their *academie* are concerts like our own, with better music and more form. Their best things are the carnival balls and masquerades, when everybody runs mad for six weeks. After their dinners and suppers, they make extempore verses and buffoon one another, but it is in a humour which you would not enter into, ye of the north.

In their houses, it is better. I should know something of the matter, having had a pretty general experience among their women, from the fisherman's wife up to the *nobil dama* whom I serve. Their system has its rules and its fitnesses, and its decorums, so as to be reduced to a kind of discipline or game at hearts, which admits few deviations, unless you wish to lose it. They are extremely tenacious, and jealous as furies, not permitting their lovers even to marry if they can help it, and keeping them always close to them in public as in private whenever they can. . . . . The reason is, they marry for their parents, and love for themselves. They exact fidelity from a lover as a debt of honor, while they pay the husband as a tradesman; that is, not at all. . . . .

Elsewhere he renders them greater justice.

With our men of letters he also made acquaintance; besides Monte and il Pellico at Milan he saw at Venice Pindemonte Ippolito; " He is a little thin man, with acute and pleasing features; his address good and gentle; his appearance altogether very philosophical; his age about 60, or more. He is one of their best going. . . . . . ."—*Memoirs*, p. 273. Letter to Murray.

The commendations of Ugo Foscolo, who, for political causes and the desire of fame, had sought tranquillity in England, whilst Byron had taken refuge in the land abandoned by Ugo, flattered him much, "because," he said, " he is a man of genius, and next because he is an Italian, &c.; besides, he's more an antique Roman than a Dane; that is, he is more of the ancient Greek than of the modern Italian. Though, somewhat, as Dugald Dalgetty says, ' too wild and salvage (like Ronald of the Mist), 'tis a wonderful man [and both my friends, Hobhouse and Rose, swear by him, &c.]' " [1] He writes again to Murray [2] :—" So you and Mr. Foscolo want me to undertake what you call a great work? An epic poem, I suppose, or some such pyramid? I'll try no such thing; I hate tasks. And then, seven or eight years! God send us well this day three months, let alone years. . . . . . And Foscolo too! Why does not he do something more than the ' Letters of Ortis,' and a tragedy and pamphlets? He has good fifteen years more at his command than I have. What has he done all that time?- -proved his genius, doubtless, but not fixed its fame, nor done his utmost, &c."

In the same letter he adds :—" If one's years can't be better employed than in writing poetry a man had better be a ditcher. And work too ! Is Childe Harold nothing? You have so many *divine* poems ; is it nothing to have written a *human* one? . . . Why, man, I could

[1] Letter to Murray, August 8, 1820.
[2] *Ibid*, April 6, 1819.

have spun the thoughts of the four cantos of that poem
into twenty . . and its passion into as many modern
tragedies, &c."

In another place he writes (3), "In general I do not
draw well with literary men; not that I dislike them,
but I never know what to say to them after I have
praised their last publication. There are several ex-
ceptions, to be sure; but then, they have either been
men of the world, such as Scott and Moore, &c., or
visionaries out of it, such as Shelley, &c.; but your
literary every-day man and I never went well in company,
especially and —— and —— and —— (I really can't
name any other). I don't remember a man amongst them
whom I ever wished to see twice, except Mezzofanti, who
is a monster of languages, the Briarœus of parts of speech,
a walking Polyglot and more, who ought to have existed
at the time of the Tower of Babel as an universal interpre-
ter. He is indeed, a marvel—unassuming also. I tried him
in all the tongues of which I knew a single oath (or adjura-
tion to the Gods against post-boys, savages, Tartars, boatmen, sailors, pilots, gondoliers, muleteers, camel-drivers,
vetturini, postmasters, post-horses, post-houses, post
everything), and, 'egad, he astounded me—even to my
English."

Elsewhere he says, however (4) : "Italy has great
names still—Canova, Monte, Ugo Foscolo, Pindemonte
Visconti, Morelli, Cicognara, Albrizzi, Mezzofanti,
Maï, Mustoxidi, Aglietti, and Vacca, will secure to the
present generation an honourable place in most of the
departments of Art, Science, and Belles Lettres, and in
some the very highest. Europe—the World—has but
one Canova."

It has been somewhere said by Alfieri, "Man is a
plant that attains to a more vigorous growth in Italy
than anywhere else—and the atrocious crimes there committed are proof of this." (5)

Without subscribing to the latter part of this propo-
sition : a dangerous doctrine, the truth of which may be
disputed on better grounds, namely, that the Italians

---

(3) *Moore*, Edition 1847 (p. 654).

(4) Dedication, Canto 4, Childe Harold.

(5) *Ibid.* See also Alfieri.

are in no respect more ferocious than their neighbours—that man must be wilfully blind, or ignorantly heedless, who is not struck with the extraordinary capacity of this people, or, if such a word be admissible, their *capabilities*, their facility of acquisition, the rapidity of their conceptions, the fire of their genius, their sense of beauty, and amidst all the disadvantages of repeated revolutions, the desolation of battle, and the despair of ages, their still unquenched longing for immortality—the immortality of independence. And we ourselves, in riding round the walls of Rome, heard the simple lament of the labourer's chorus: "Roma! Roma! Roma! Roma non è più come era prima!" &c.

Byron was amongst the few foreigners who distrusted not our national valour. "The courage of the French," he said, "springs from vanity, that of the Germans from phlegm, the Turk's from fanaticism and opium, the Spaniard's from pride, that of the English from a cold temperament; but the courage of the Italians arises from anger."

He also studied deeply the Italian language, translated into his own tongue the episode of Francesca da Rimini, and (on which he plumed himself greatly) the first canto of the Morgante Maggiore, verse for verse; and he said that if he lived nine or ten years longer (which he doubted), having become versed in Italian, he would have composed in that tongue his best work.

And this future, *in prospectu*, he greatly caressed, promising that he would then have done things at which the world would have been amazed. He now also became disturbed in his imagination by a presentiment which announced to him his approaching end, or by thoughts of the warfare to which from time to time he was excited by his aristocratic companions, who alternately lauded to the skies and levelled to the dust his poetic compositions.

And thus it was that from happy dreams of fame he often awoke in disgust, and inscribed in his diary: "The only pleasure of fame is that it paves the way to pleasure; and the more intellectual our pleasure the better for the pleasure and for us too."

Afterwards, travelling one day from Florence to Pisa,
he composed the verses, commencing :—

> Oh ! talk not to me of a name great in story,
> The days of our youth are the days of our glory ;
> And the myrtle and ivy of sweet two-and-twenty
> Are worth all your laurels, thongh ever so plenty. . . &c.

But can we believe him ? Fame yet flattered (and how
greatly flattered !) the poet ; and not seldom was it a
happiness to him. With what satisfaction do we find
him describing an American lady who at Leghorn took
from him a rose, saying that she wished to carry away
with her to the other hemisphere something that had
belonged to so great a poet. How transparent his joy
through the affected disparagement with which he dis-
cussed the eulogies awarded him by the American
journals. In Scotland, an outbreak occurring, the rioters
resolved to cross the lands of Byron, but in single file
only, so as to open merely a pathway through his
estate, whilst they consigned to destruction his neighbours' property. Thus did genius extort consideration
for its superiority over rank and wealth ([6]).

XXVII.

PROCEEDS TO GREECE.

But Lord Byron had been always persuaded that man
was bound to do more for society than make verses.
When still a boy, he was accustomed to say, " I will
some day or other raise a troop, the men of which shall
be dressed in black and ride on black horses. They shall
be called 'Byron's Blacks,' and you will hear of their
performing prodigies of valour ([1])." And the moment is
now come to realise that dream. After so many poems
and some prose writings, so much said in Parliament,
and such articles in journals, so many dithyrambic
lamentations, and so much lukewarm enthusiasm seen
and heard for Greece, what could be more to Byron's·

([6]) In this anecdote usually known ?—Ed.
([1]) *Moore's Life.*

heart than to go to its aid? Nor did he go there dazzled
by that poetic ardour which had led him to depict so
to the life the fervid regions of the East. Too well, indeed,
he knew the difficulties of the case; without treasure,
without allies, without laws, and, worse than all, without
union; threatened by superior force, yet, like Curtius,
who precipitated himself into the gulf where he knew
he must perish, he does not recoil from exposing himself to the risk of so many mishaps, and for it he
abandons Italy, this beautiful Italy, and a mistress.
He embraced his friends. "Something within tells me,"
he said, "that I may not again return from Greece,"
and he wept. He turned to her he loved. The fair
Italian mingled her grief with his, and would have
followed him; but, feeble in health as she still was,
Byron would not consent.

On the 14th of July, the "Hercules" (²) set sail for
Greece; the sacred shores of Italy faded from the
poet's sight: the sea, his ancient companion, exults
around the ship, like a steed which knows its rider.

> Roll on, thou deep and dark blue ocean, roll,
> Ten thousand fleets sweep over thee in vain;
> Man marks the earth with ruin, his control
> Stops with the shore; upon the watery plain
> The wrecks are all thy deed, nor doth remain
> A shadow of man's ravage, save his own,
> When for a moment, like a drop of rain,
> He sinks into thy depths, with bubbling groan,
> Without a grave, unknell'd, uncoffin'd, and unknown. . &c.

Thus he sails over the Ionian sea, in rocky Ithaca
visits the grotto of Ulysses and there is lulled to sleep.
He bathes in the baths of Penelope and takes his repast
at Arethusa's fountains. At Chios, over the wretched
ruins which are still named the School of Homer, he
enters into a long discourse with an aged bishop who had
there sought to recover his health. Alas! what joy
reigns throughout unhappy Greece, when the people learn
that Byron has arrived; that the poet has come in their
defence. Again return to their minds the days of
triumphant art. Hail to the new Tyrtœus! Here
he diffuses his beneficence around him, he quenches
tears, he succours want, supports tottering old age; his
name is held in veneration. A few days after his

(²) Commanded by Captain Scott.

arrival, he receives from the mountains of Agrafa this missive : " Your letter and that of the venerable Ignazio have filled me with joy. Your Excellency is exactly the person whom we need. Let nothing prevent you from coming into this part of Greece. The enemy threatens us in great numbers, but, by the help of God and your Excellency, they shall meet a suitable resistance. I shall have something to do to-night against a corps of 6,000 or 7,000 Albanians, encamped close to this place. The day after to-morrow I will set out, with a few chosen companions, to meet your Excellency. Do not delay. I thank you for the good opinion you have of my fellow-citizens, which God grant you will not find ill-founded ; and I thank you still more for the care you have so kindly taken of them." Know you by whom this letter was written ? By Marco Bozzaris (³) ; and written upon the day on the night of which he was to shed his blood for the cause of Christ and his country.

XXVIII.

RELIGIOUS BELIEF.

Byron having come with the declared object of fighting, under the banner of Christ, amidst a people who, in the very savageness of their nature, feel to the heart's core the enthusiasm of religion, and display it in their rites, their songs, their mode of life, what moment could have been more opportune for a return of thoughts to things above, which, throughout life, he appeared to have forgotten ! Not that he would be an Atheist ; he had himself many times declared the falsehood of that assertion ; but, even in his heart, indifference stagnated—indifference, the most common evil of our state of being. Most affectionate is the prayer which a pious lady from Hastings addressed to the Deity, that

(3). In a night attack against the Turks, Bozzaris afterwards fell.

in his mercy he would reclaim the soul of the poet, in whom forgetfulness of God was nearly as great, perhaps, as were the gifts of genius he had received from heaven ; and that He would teach him to seek, in the comforts of religion, that peace of mind which the world and its vanities cannot give. At which prayer, when brought to Byron's knowledge by the husband of the deceased lady, Byron was touched to the quick. Here is an extract from his letter to Mr. Sheppard :—" Indisputably, the firm believers in the Gospel have a great advantage over all others, for this simple reason, that, if true, they will have their reward—hereafter, and if there be no hereafter, they can but be with the infidel in his eternal sleep, having had the assistance of an exalted hope through life, without subsequent disappointment, since (to the worst of them), ' out of nothing, nothing can arise,' not even sorrow. I can assure you that all the fame which ever cheated humanity into higher notions of its own importance, would never weigh in my mind against the pure and pious interest which a virtuous being may be pleased to take in my welfare. I would not exchange the prayer of the deceased in my behalf for the united glory of Homer, Cæsar, and Napoleon, could such be accumulated upon a living heart. Do me at least the justice to suppose, that ' Video meliora proboque,' however the ' deteriora sequor' may have been applied to my conduct.—BYRON." (1)

We have seen how Walter Scott predicted to him that he would end by turning to Catholicism ; and, in fact, to the Roman Catholic faith, towards the end of his days, he more than inclined. His natural daughter (Allegra), who, dying shortly after, left him almost inconsolable, he had placed for education in the Convent of Bagno Cavallo, that she might there imbibe religious ideas ; and, said he :—" It is, besides, my wish that she should be a Roman Catholic, which I look upon as the best religion, as it is the oldest, assuredly, of the branches of Christianity." The bold ideas on the ancient world and the religious opinions which he vauntingly put forth in Cain, he declared to his friends were not his own, but he had been obliged to identify himself with his

(1). Letter to Mr. Sheppard, Pisa, December 8, 1821.　　F 2

personages, according as they were Abel or Lucifer, Cain or Adam. "I am no enemy to religion, but the contrary. As a proof, I am educating my natural daughter a strict Catholic in a Convent of Romagna; for I think people can never have enough of religion if they are to have any. I incline myself very much to the Catholic doctrines; but, if I am to write a drama, I must make my characters speak as I conceive them likely to argue (2)."

Arrived in Greece, during the hours of liberty that the duties of the cause for which he was to fight allowed him, he held conversations with Dr. Kennedy, who had charged himself with the task of making him a good Christian, and of him he demanded the solution of things of which he was still doubtful in mind. The relation of these colloquies is most curious. To the faith he was disposed to give to the Holy Scriptures he opposed the opinions of the few men he had met who could have had a firm and conscientious belief. Every day he read the Bible he asked his preceptor, "Then you still think me in a very bad way. . . . I am, however, in a fairer way. I already believe in predestination, which I know you believe, and in the depravity of the human heart in general, and of my own in particular. . . . I shall get at the others bye and bye, &c." And, reasoning on a work of Dr. Southwood on the "Divine Government," he says: "I cannot decide the point; but, to my present apprehension, it would be a most desirable thing could it be proved that ultimately all created beings were happy. This would appear to be most consistent with God, whose power is omnipotent, and whose chief attribute is Love, &c."

And the God of Love, let us hope, will have gathered to his bosom and to that peace which here below is never enjoyed, a soul so profoundly inspired by his creative breath. (1) Thus much do we dwell upon the setting of that star which, now moving in a new sphere of action and of virtue, shone with greater lustre when just about to be extinguished.

(2). Letter to Moore (No. 482), 1847, Pisa, March, 1822.

XXIX.

HIS DEATH.

Unhappy Greece ! Byron had courted it in the bright-est dreams of his verse ; and now beheld it in the most deplorable abandonment and distress. On every side disunion—all leaders, not one a soldier : torn by factions in turns ; a dearth of treasure and of counsel, against an ever-increasing foe ; no other defence than mountains, rivers, marshes, and men's hearts. Misso-longhi threatened ; the Suliotes, armed and all powerful, demand pay and pay there is not : the fleet dispersed ; artillery who refused to serve their guns. The rest, who, if worse could be, alas ! were even worse. Amid such, Byron all but alone to lavish wealth and life, to scatter the accumulations of his economy (he had been, 'twas said, a miser), the produce of his works and his credit, and yet without deceiving himself as to the result of an unreasonable warfare. All the qualities of a good soldier he possessed : courage, hardihood, coolness, humanity. Conducting affairs in a liberal and compas-sionate spirit, he succeeded in checking, both amongst his own followers and among the Turks, the commission of acts of ruthless barbarity in an art of itself murderous, however pompous and high-sounding the names with which the sophisms of the ambitious may bedeck it. To Greece, therefore, he appeared more than mortal. By him that herdsman's hut, destroyed by fire, was rebuilt ; through him that fatherless family found bread, and an honoured existence ; by him that soldier, that troop, that entire ship, was saved from the ruthless hands of the Turks, to whom he had given lessons and exampes in generosity. On one occasion, his vessel is delayed It is made known that she is in the hands of the Turks, and the consternation is universal. At last, she comes, she comes ! At the momentous intelligence, all Miss-olonghi crowd the shore. The guns from the fortress and ships in harbour salute the happy return ; all the troops, all the officials, with Mavrocordato at their head, receive her with acclamations and salvoes of artillery, according to their custom, bands of music accompanying the national air, " δευτε παιδες των 'Ελληνων."

Conceive, then, the universal lamentation when it is known that fatigues of the body, or rather those of the mind, had overwhelmed him; that he was ill, growing worse; that he was at the point of death! Death had more than once summoned him; had, as it is said, more than once tried to accelerate its approach, on some one of those days of sorrow when grief itself is cherished to fill the mind's void. Now, when the time of action had arrived, when his powerful will, amid so many obstacles, found at length a scope whereon to direct the combination of virtue, of genius, and of glory, Byron, far from his country, his friends, his mistress, his Ada—Byron, at thirty-six years of age, died.

The physicians knew not at first his malady; then, he refused their prescriptions, nor would he again allow them to draw blood from him until too late. The last day of his life, Fletcher, his own faithful valet, attended him; to whom, feeling himself at the point of death, he strove to explain his last wishes.

" Shall I fetch pens and paper?" said the latter to him.

" Oh! no," replied the dying man, " there is no time; it is now nearly over—go to my sister Augusta—tell her —go to Lady Byron—you will see her, and say—"

Here his voice faltered, and became gradually indistinct; notwithstanding which, he still continued to murmur to himself for nearly twenty minutes with much earnestness of manner, but in such a tone that only a few words could be distinguished. These, too, were only names—" Augusta "—" Ada "—" Hobhouse "—" Kinnaird." He then said, " Now I have told you all." " My Lord," replied Fletcher, " I have not understood a word your Lordship has been saying." " Not understand me?" exclaimed Lord Byron, with a look of the most intense distress." " What a pity!—then it is too late, all is over." " I hope not," answered Fletcher, " but the Lord's will be done."

He then tried to utter a few words, of which none were intelligible, except " My sister, my child."

It was the 19th of April, 1824, the Day of Passover, of devout rejoicing, but the hymn was unheard in the desolate city of Missolonghi; the cry of exultation— " Christ is risen"—rested unspoken on the lips—the churches were crowded with people who propitiated the Deity; no other question was asked by those who met, but " How is Lord Byron?" At a quarter past six in the evening, a furious whirlwind swept over the city. The affrighted inhabitants rushed in crowds from their homes, in their superstitious grief exclaiming " The great man is gone."

He opened his eyes once again, and then closed them for ever.

XXX.

THE GENERAL GRIEF.

Throughout the land was one universal sob of grief, of discouragement; Greece honored the hero, the benefactor, the fellow-soldier; they were not aware, poor Greeks , how much they should lament the poet. At his obsequies, celebrated on the Thursday after his death, Spiridione Tricoupi addressed the assembled multitude. Overcome with sincere grief, and interrupted by no mercenary lamentations, he summed up the virtues of the deceased, concluding thus: " When your exertions, my friends, shall have liberated us from the hands which have so long held us down in chains; from the hands which have torn from us our arms, our property, our brothers, our children, then will his spirit rejoice, then will his shade be satisfied ! Yes, in that blessed hour of our freedom, the Archbishop will extend his sacred and free hand, and pronounce a blessing over his venerated tomb ; the young warrior, sheathing his sword, red with the blood of his tyrannical oppressors, will bedeck it with laurel; the statesman will consecrate it with his oratory, and the poet, upon the marble, will become doubly inspired; virgins of Greece (whose beauty our illustrious fellow-citizen Byron has celebrated in so many of his poems) without fearing any longer contamination from the rapacious hands of our oppressors, crowning their heads with garlands,

will dance around it and sing of the beauty of our land
which the poet of our age, has already commemorated with
such grace and truth. But what sorrowful thought now
presses upon my mind. My fancy has carried me away.
I had imagined the blessings of our bishops, the hymns
and laurel crowns, and the dance of the virgins of
Greece around the tomb of the benefactor of Greece,
—but this tomb will not contain his precious remains,
will remain void. For a few days only will his
body remain on the face of our land—of his chosen
country; it cannot be given to us; it must be borne
to his own, his native, land which is honoured
by his birth. Oh! daughter most dearly beloved by
him, your arms will receive him, your tears will
bathe the tomb which shall contain his body : and
the tears of the orphans of Greece will be shed over
the urn containing his precious heart. Missolonghi, his
country, will ever watch over and protect with all her
strength the urn containing his venerated heart, as a
symbol of his love towards us. All Greece, clothed in
mourning, and inconsolable, accompanies the procession,
in which it is to be borne; all ecclesiastical, civil, and military honors attend it. . . Learn, noble lady, learn that
chieftains bore it on their shoulders, and carried it to
the church ; thousands of Greek soldiers lined the way
through which it passed, with their muskets, which had
destroyed so many tyrants, pointed towards the ground.
. . . . All this crowd of soldiers, ready to march at a
moment against the implacable enemy of Christ and
man, surrounded the funeral car, and swore never to
forget the sacrifices made by your father for us, and
never to allow the spot where his heart is placed to be
trampled upon by barbarous and tyrannical feet.
Thousands of Christian voices were in a moment heard,
and the temple of the Almighty resounded with supplica-
tions and prayers that his venerated remains might be
safely conveyed to his native land, and that his soul
might rest where the righteous alone find rest."

The urn was in fact raised upon the walls of Missolonghi, those walls which were ere long to fall in ruins,
sacrificed by its own citizens, as Byron had sacrificed
his own existence.

Along every shore of the Archipelago were celebrated the hero's funeral rites. Lepanto taken, the Greek warriors consecrated one of its bastions to their fellow-soldier, thrice inscribing it with his name. The Governor decreed him the title of Father of the Nation ; a title than which none could be more illustrious, were it not sometimes the guerdon of adulation or of cowardice. The daughter of Byron was likewise addressed in the language of Homer.

As, in ancient times, the ashes of Themistocles were carried back to Athens, so the remains of the poet, after being embalmed, were conveyed to London. There, for some days, the body lay exposed to the view of the multitude. The indignation against him had ceased. England laid aside her haughty pride, and turned with eagerness to honour with her tears and eulogies the remains of the great poet, who, in his lifetime, she had persecuted. With a funeral cortège suitable to such a man and such a country, he was borne to his ancestral vault at Newstead, and the torch of fame, as happens oft, blazed most brilliantly beside the sepulchre.

XXXI.

HIS CHARACTER.

It is maintained that the character of Byron is to be recognised in the heroes of his compositions; in the dizziness of Manfred's intellectual ambition; in the sated dissipation of Childe Harold, who tears himself from social life through craving for material activity ; in Lara, who vainly strives to stifle the remorse of a soul steeped in crime, but cannot. He has been converted into a Don Juan, even a Cain. And truly, in these portraitures, here and there, he has left some traits which appear to reveal, under the hero's mask, the author (1). The wicked indubitably wish not to reveal their own misdeeds, though an exaggerated contempt for public opinion may indeed cause them to let others believe of them both vices and crimes. Certainly, regarding Byron strange things were told; the most extraordinary adventures in his travels were related of him; that he was stained with the guilt of assassination—killing a husband who had sacrificed a faithless wife. In all his writings was discernible, it was said, an habitual tinge of blood; a remorse which continued to persecute him. Who could interrogate his ashes? We know well, indeed, that having declared open war upon many classes of society, in a satire more poignant perhaps than true, the latter were ready to oppose his shafts by lowering the poet in public estimation. But how comes it that of a man who ever, from his youth upwards, had fixed upon him the scrutinizing eye of envy and admiration, these offences could never be proved—the time or place given? On the other hand, in his very first stanzas, occurs this tinge of remorse, this note of woe from the man who found himself under the ban of condemnation. Strange singularity! The poet who ever showed himself so deeply sensitive to the censure of his works, affected to heed little, or not at all, those directed against his character, and he not so much neglected only as he defied public opinion. To his romantic fancy it was perhaps pleasing to see himself held up as a being different from his fellow-men, at a time when civilization levelled all grades : he trusted, moreover, that his works would speak for him, that after his death his whole soul would be revealed in the memorials entrusted to the dearest of his friends—Poor Byron! The very confidence with which he relied on a friend best reveals his innermost soul.

To those around him, indeed, he was affectionate and compassionate. To his mother, his sister Augusta, his daughter, he displayed ever the most cordial affection : with domestics kind, so that he rendered them entirely devoted to him; even to animals (a thing not to be overlooked) he was humane, and most particular affection he bore to a dog, whose death he deplored in verse. (2) Amid the babble of crowded assemblies he was discouraged and kept himself apart; nor wonder was it, since, on his appearance in society, all eyes were fixed upon him, every lip repeated his name ; he was sensible of being, as it were, on the stage, where his every word was noted. But, when he found himself among a few trusted friends, you could not imagine how sincere the full expansion of his heart, how truly great his generous hospitality. The charge of misanthropy displeased him, yet in reality there was visible in him, if not scorn, yet an inclination to avoid society ; and this, at first vague and general, afterwards, amid the persecutions and woes caused by others' perversity, became personal antipathy.

> I have not loved the world, nor the world me (1) ;
>   I have not flatter'd its rank breath, nor bow'd
> To its idolatries a patient knee.
>   Nor coin'd my cheek in smiles—nor cried aloud
>   In worship of an echo ; in the crowd
> They could not deem me one of such ; I stood
>   Among them, but not of them ; in a shroud
> Of thoughts which were not their thoughts, and still could,
> Had I not filed my mind, which thus itself subdued.
>
> I have not loved the world, nor the world me—
>   But let us part fair foes ; I do believe,
> Though I have found them not, that there may be
>   Words which are things—hopes which will not deceive,
>   And virtues which are merciful, nor weave
> Snares for the falling, &c.

Lines such as these portray his feelings : even to his native land he declared his hatred ; but there, he ever retained his dearest friends : no Englishman approached his presence who received not from him the most perfect courtesy.

> Yet was I born where men are proud to be,
>   Not without cause ; and should I leave behind
> The inviolate island of the sage and free,
> And seek me out a home by a remoter sea,
>   Perhaps I loved it well ; and should I lay
> My ashes in a soil which is not mine ;
> My spirit shall resume it—if we may
> Unbodied choose a sanctuary (2). . . . . . .

His benevolence studied only the opportunity of being exercised with delicacy : he also had suffered. Many times he smoothed with his largesses the young students' path : to young girls who could not marry for want of means he awarded a sufficient dowry. At Venice, they will tell you of his benefactions ; a poor fisherman's hut was destroyed, and he caused it to be rebuilt ; a printer's work-shop was burned, and he liberally assisted him. And with heart-felt delight he

(1) 4th Canto, Childe Harold.
(2) 4th Canto, Childe Harold.

related his charity to an aged female who, in her gratitude, knew no better return to make him than a bunch of spring violets, which he cherished most dearly. When political events endangered the tranquillity of his residence at Ravenna, the poor of the place petitioned the Legate there that he would be pleased to entreat Lord Byron to remain, and guarantee his security.

At Cefalonia, an embankment fell in, burying the workmen with it : Byron learns it, hurries to the spot, and, seeing that the operation of disinterring the sufferers is proceeding slowly, reproves the workmen, even chastises them, and himself gives a hand to rescue the unfortunates from their entombment.

Nor, without indignation, could he contemplate the wrongs inflicted on humanity ; and hence it was that he would never forgive the egotistical misdeeds of his country, in trafficking with every people and every nation. In Athens, when he first resided there, he sees a young girl who had been guilty of an intercourse with a Christian, whom the Turks (according to custom) were about to cast into the sea. Byron, first with arguments, then with threats, and finally with pistol in hand, induced the Governor to desist from his legalised atrocity, and to consign to him the delinquent, whom he then placed in a convent.

Afterwards, when he repaired to Greece, there to find the most glorious of tombs—a soldier's grave—he used every effort to instil into the Hellenes all the humanity compatible with war, the scourge of God, and justified only by absolute necessity.

On his arrival, he fell in with a Turk who had but just escaped from the hands of some Greek sailors ; he gives him refuge in his own house, and protests to his incensed pursuers that while he lived they should do him no injury, Some Turkish prisoners incarcerated at Missolonghi he sends to the Pacha Yussuf, entreating him, for pity's sake, that he would henceforth refrain from the useless execution of his captives.

The freedom of twenty-four captive women and children he obtained also, and, sending them to Prevesa, wrote to the English Consul there on their behalf :—[3]

(3) Letter to Mr. Meyer.—*Moore,* 1847, p. 623.

" Coming to Greece, one of my principal objects was to
alleviate as much as possible the miseries incident to a
warfare as cruel as the present. When the dictates
of humanity are in question, I know no difference
between Turks and Greeks. . . . . . The best
recompense I can hope for would be to find that I had
inspired the Ottoman commanders with the same
sentiments towards those unhappy Greeks who may
hereafter fall into their hands."

With such splendid qualities was Byron happy ? Did he
rightly fulfil the high mission of a great man upon earth ?
In truth is it that, considering the misfortunes of the poet,
man is consoled amid his own unhappiness ; and therefore, it appears that nothing could have been more
injurious to him than the superfluity of his own means.
Had he grown to manhood in the narrow circumstances
in which he was born, we should have found him compelled to struggle with necessity, the stimulus of the
strong ; then, having overcome difficulties, raising himself
to eminence, in peace with himself and the human race.
Had he found a country to conquer, a path to open for
himself in the midst of tumult, a cause for which to
triumph, either in the tribune or in the camp, as general
or as deputy, he would have attained the highest success,
for he possessed all the necessary qualifications. He
would perhaps have added to the too infrequen,
miracles of the human race ; but the sudden wealth
acquired without an effort in his youth, soon changed
his nature, and those who, in educating a boy, should
have paid attention to his heart, in educating a lord,
neglected morality, or looked only to the intellect.
We know not if it has befallen anyone on his way
through life, to find himself the sport of every mishap,
to experience a multitude of failures, a myriad of desires,
a void unfilled by a variety of objects, a longing for rest
even there. It appears that this was exactly Byron's
case. From his family he was, as it were, a branch cut
off; he could not hope for the felicity of domestic affection,
the welcome of a father returning to his home, a welcome
to which all that the proud monarch and the conqueror
receive is but the shadow of a shade. From his country
he exiled himself, as likewise from the whole human race ;

whilst, in order to excuse himself, he was interested in depicting man as wicked. Far from those whose voice, even presence, would have sufficed to bring him back to the right path, he is to be pitied if he strayed, if, abandoned by every soothing thought, he was driven to phrensy—

> Why marvel ye if they who lose
> This present joy, this future hope,
> No more with sorrow meekly cope,
> In phrensy then their fate accuse. (4) . . &c.

—if, in fine, in tasting pleasure after pleasure, he sought that forgetfulness he had in vain invoked from domestic consolations. And, when he pours forth the blackness of his choler in loud notes of woe, the poignancy of which he loved to exaggerate to himself, the query comes to the lips which the Abbot put to Manfred ; " And why not live, and act with other men.? "

Whenever, in fact, he approached real life, mingled with his equals, made acquaintance with real wants, virtues, vices, and sufferings, and not through the medium of a deceitful prism, he then became a man capable of every virtue, and the poet of truth. Intercourse with Italians, all his biographers confess, effected great good, in restoring his mind to tranquillity and a right train of thought. " His genius," observes a discerning writer, " needed the necessity of managing and discussing his own affairs." Certain it is that had he returned from Greece his genius would have largely expanded. In striving to effect an union between Mavrocordato and Colocotroni, (5) he would have acquired actual acquaintance with the human heart ; then, perchance, he would have been enabled to raise himself to the sublimity of real tragedy, he would have suffered less from misanthropy, nor dwelt upon the thought how much that surrounded him was occupied with him, and that only to envy or to deceive him. Thus, as it were, betrayed, he turned upon the whole human race his glance of scorn and of desperation : then, strove to drown thought in pleasure. But pleasure could not suffice a mind like his. Action he needed, the necessity of action he felt ; and whilst he would have wished to find it in influencing

(4) The Giaour.
(5) The two leaders of the Greeks.

the destinies of his country, he felt ever a condition of
inferiority of position, beyond which he had not even the
hope of a disaster.   Hence the weariness of existence,—
the most incurable of the mind's maladies—assailed him.

> It is not love, it is not hate,
> Nor low ambition's honors lost,
> That bids me loathe my present state,
> And fly from all I prized the most;
>
> It is that weariness which springs
> From all I meet, or hear, or see;
> To me no pleasure beauty brings,
> Thine eyes have scarce a charm for me (6) . . &c.

The moment of action at length came : he appeared
then great as he really was,—and then—he died.

XXXII.

CONCLUDING SUMMARY.

But this ennui, this weariness of existence, is a malady
too common in our age.   It may be seen consuming the
Italian in his siesta, and it makes havoc with the
Parisian in the vortex of his pleasures.   In vain is it to
strive to avoid it in the whirl of thought or the maddening enjoyment of dissipation.   It enters the gilded
palace, the voluptuous boudoir, mingles with the exultation of the dance, is seated at the most sumptuous
banquets, accompanies the joys of love, and attaches
itself especially to the imprudent who would eschew or
neglect its real remedy.   Is there not for every human
being a sublime goal on which to direct his efforts? Have
we not a family, a country? Is there not assigned to us a
position, a post, in the ways of life? That post let us not
vilely desert, either through flattery or through threats.
Beyond that is weariness, is discontent, the mournful
inheritance of impotence.   But brotherly love, the
soothing effect of influence, this is the fount whence
consolation and comfort most abundantly flow.

Thus have we endeavoured to trace the lineaments of

(6) *Childe Harold*, Canto 1.

a great man, because we believe that there is more
instruction in the errors of great men than in the more
ordinary miseries of the human race.   What influence
had he upon society?   Should morality or taste cut
short the newly essayed chord which he attached to his
lyre?   Is the great poet or the benevolent citizen to be
imitated, or are we to bewail only the misguided
libertine?   Those whom the bitter disenchantment of
experience has taught to separate from the mere mass
that bright substance —the fire of generosity which shines
so brightly in the eyes of youth : those in whose mind
is exhausted, along with the source of evil that also of
good, will find too much for which to condemn the poet
and the man.   Should we not desire rather there to ,
seek a lesson?   Evenness of disposition, my readers,
peace of mind, the interchange of benefits and of
benevolent actions, are a happiness that Byron, in the
aggregate, knew not.

He was unable to reside in his own country, because
to live there, in his proper sphere, he must have been of
use to it, he must have exerted himself.   Now, how can
he exert himself worthily who abandons himself a prey
to doubt?   A great persuasion, an absolute confidence, can
alone be our guide to worthy and successful efforts.
Unhappy he, who, like Byron, sacrifices his peace of
mind to discouraging doubt ; imprudent the man who,
from the study of letters, seeks his own eulogy, not the
general weal ; who receives not the gift of genius from
on high, a mission to mankind, a social, a patriotic
mission.   Byron, it is true, brought into his compositions
a freedom of thought which rendered him independent
of the petty desires, the mean animosities, of coteries ;
but then, he sacrificed to his own antipathies and to
his own sympathies.

Vice, indeed, he could not depict as enviable ; he
never depicted felicity as resulting from the sway of the
passions ; he preached not egotism ; but the continual
creation of the ideal of vice may habituate man to it ; if
he combatted sin, yet he did not confidently defend
virtue.   Nor is abstinence from evil enough, when we
wish to excite to virtue, to the noble sentimens
which adorn mankind.   And yet Byron had written :—"In

my mind, the highest of all poetry is ethical poetry, as the highest of all earthly subjects must be moral truth. Religion does not make a part of our subjects; it is something beyond human powers, and has failed in all human hands except Milton's and Dante's, and even Dante is involved in his delineations of human passions, though in supernatural circumstances. What made Socrates the greatest man? His moral truth, his ethics. What proved Jesus Christ the Son of God, hardly less than His miracles—His moral precepts?" Thus Byron wrote, but in fact, if he had considered the internal voice which interprets what in us is divine, he would not so often have sacrificed genius to caprice, to doubt, to sarcasm, to personal resentment. Oh! had he but laboured to a greater end; oh! had he but poured forth lamentations useful to the real griefs of humanity! Alas! we can but deplore! To reclaim the past is beyond our powers!

NOTES.

CHAPTER I.

(1.)

" Lord Byron was descended from an illustrious line of ancestry. From the period of the Conquest, his family, who possessed extensive manors in Lancashire and other parts of the kingdom, were highly distinguished for their prowess in arms. . . . Two fell at Cressy . . . another fought at Bosworth. Seven sons of Sir John Byron fought at Marston Moor on the king's side, and four fell in defence of the royal cause. Sir John, one of the survivors, was created Lord Byron, October 26, 1643. . . . William, Lord Byron, in 1763, was made Master of the Staghounds, and in 1765 was sent to the Tower for killing Mr. Chaworth in a duel. . . . . John, next brother to William, accompanied Lord Anson in his voyages, and his narratives of his sufferings and the hardships encountered he is well known. " Mad Jock Byron," of the Guards, celebrated for his beauty, and notorious for his dissipation, was his son, and born in 1751. He married Miss Catherine Gordon, an Aberdeenshire heiress, and lineal descendant from the Earl of Huntley and Princess Jane, daughter of James I. Having run through his property, he left her and his only child, and retired to Valenciennes, where he died in 1791. This was Byron's father—the poet, George Gordon Byron having been born at Dover," &c.—(Abridged from *Bulwer's Life*).

(2)

" Newstead Abbey was founded in 1170 by Henry II., as a Priory of Black Canons, and dedicated to the Virgin Mary. It continued in the family till the time of the poet, who sold it to Mr. Claughton for £140,000, who, failing in his agreement, and paying £20,000 forfeit, it was sold again, and most of the proceeds vested in trustees for the jointure of the Hon. Mrs. Byron." . . . Walpole says, " I saw both Newstead and Althorp. I like both, the former is the very Abbey. The great east window remains. . . . the hall entire—the refectory entire, the cloisters untouched. . . . it has a private chapel, quite perfect. In the park, which is still charming, £5,000 worth of the timber (old oaks) were cut by the old lord. . . . In the hall is a very good collection of pictures, all animals. The refectory, now the great drawing room, is full of Byrons, the vaulted roof remaining, but the windows have new dresses making for them by a Venetian tailor."

—From Bulwer's Life.

CHAPTER II.

(1.)

" My epitaph shall be my name alone
If that with honour fail to crown my clay,
Oh ! may no other fame my deeds repay !
That, only that, shall single out the spot,
By that remember'd, or with that forgot." *

* " Childish Recollections," as printed in first unpublished volume :—
" Oft when oppress'd with sad, foreboding gloom,
I sat reclined upon our favorite tomb."

(3)

Vide Virgil, Ecl. 3 v. 90. Horace, 10th Epode, v. 2.

Mœvius was an obscure poet, of the time of Augustus, whose envious diatribes on Virgil and others of celebrity amongst the famous of that day, gained him an unenviable notoriety.—ED.

(4)

Elsewhere he says (Medwin, p. 213) :—" When I first saw the review of my 'Hours of Idleness' (1808), I was furious; in such a rage as I never have been in since. I dined that day with Scrope Davies, and drank three bottles of claret to drown it, but it only boiled the more," &c.

On the first leaf of the copy retained by himself, now in Mr. Murray's possession, he had written:—"The binding of this volume is considerably too valuable for its contents. Nothing but the consideration of its being the property of another prevents me from consigning the miserable record of misplaced anger and indiscriminate acrimony to the flames."—Letter to Harness, 1809, *Moore's Life.*

CHAPTER III.

(1)

Letter of C. S. Matthews to Miss T. M., May 22, 1809.—*Moore's Life,* 1847. "We went down to Newstead together, where I had got a famous cellar, and monks dressed from a masquerade warehouse. We were a company of some 7 or 8, with an occasional neighbour or so, for a visitor, and used to sit up late in our friars' dresses, drinking burgundy, claret, champagne, and what not, out of the skull cup, and all sorts of glasses. . . Matthews always denominated me the 'Abbot';" &c.—*Moore's Life,* p. 60. Letter to Murray, Ravenna, Nov. 12, 1820.

(2)

Lines on a Cup formed from a Skull (Miscellaneous Poems).*

* (Goethe's *Faust*). And from *Faust* we have:—
" Why dost thou grin at me, grim empty skull ?
Is't that thy brain, like mine. mistook its way ?
Seeking for noonday in the twilight dull—
Lusting for truth, went wretchedly astray ? "

CHAPTER IV.

(1)

"The Earl of Carlisle (his Guardian*) having declined to introduce him to the House of Lords, he resolved to introduce himself, and accordingly went there a little before the usual hour, when he knew few of the Lords would be present. On entering he appeared rather abashed, and looked very pale, but passing the Woolsack, where the Chancellor (Lord Eldon) was engaged in some of the ordinary routine of the House, he went directly to the table, where the oaths were administered to him. The Lord Chancellor then approached, and offered his hand in the most friendly manner, congratulating him on his taking possession of his seat. Lord Byron only placed the tips of his fingers in the Chancellor's hand. The latter returned to his seat, and Byron, after lounging a few minutes on one of the Opposition benches, retired. To Mr. Dallas, who followed him out, he gave, as a reason for not entering into the spirit of the Chancellor, 'that it might have been supposed he would join the Court party, whereas he intended to have nothing at all to do with politics.' He only addressed the House three times. The first of his speeches was on the Framework Bill, the second in favour of the Catholic claims, which gave good hopes of his becoming an orator, and the other related to a petition from Major Cartwright. Byron himself says, 'The Lords told him his manner was not dignified enough for them, and would better suit the Lower House.' Others say they gathered round him while speaking, listening with the greatest attention—a sign, at any rate, that he was interesting. He always voted with the Opposition, but evinced no

* The Earl's father having married the preceeding Lady Byron, Isabella, a poetess, who afterwards secluded herself from the world.

likelihood of becoming the partisan of either side."—*Life by Sir H. L. Bulwer*, 1831; *Johnson's Lives of the Poets, &c.*

CHAPTER VI.

(1)

Amongst the many portraits of Byron the most true to life is that of Phillips, finely lithographed by Senefelder. Thorwaldsen's bust of the poet is mean.

"Thorwaldsen has done a bust of me at Rome for Mr. Hobhouse, which is reckoned very good. He is their best after Canova, and by some preferred to him."—Letter to Murray, Venice, June 4, 1817.

(2)

The fashionable dentist of Old Bond Street. "Went," says the *Byron Journal*, 1814, "to Waite. Teeth all right and white, but he says that I grind them in my sleep, and chip the edges."

(3)

Of Blake he writes :

"Write but like Wordsworth, live beside a lake,
  And keep your bushy locks a year from Blake."

"As famous a tonsor as Licinius himself, and better paid, and may like him be one day a Senator, having a better qualification than one half of the heads he crops—viz., independence."—"Hints from Horace," *Byron's Works.*

(4)

Madame Albrizzi (Ritratti).

"I never walked down St. Mark's by moonlight without thinking of the 'Ghost Seer,' by Schiller, &c."—Letter to Murray, Venice, April 2.

(5)

"Since our last meeting I am reduced 4st. in weight. I then weighed 14½st., and now only 10½st. I have disposed of my superfluities by means of hard exercise and abstinence."—Letter to Mr. Drury, Dorant's Hotel, January 13, 1808.

CHAPTER VIII.

(1)

" Well, thou art happy, and I feel
  That I should thus be happy too :
For still my heart regards thy weal,
  Warmly as it was wont to do.

Thy husband's blest—and 'twill impart
  Some pangs to view his happier lot :
But let them pass—Oh! how my heart
  Would hate him, if he loved thee not!

When late I saw thy favorite child,
  I thought my jealous heart would break ;
But when the unconscious infant smiled
  I kissed it for its mother's sake." &c.

CHAPTER X.

(1)

When Ariosto first showed his verses to the Cardinal d' Este, the latter is said to have replied :—*Dove, diavolo, Messire Ludovico, avese pigliato tante coglionerie?* "Where the devil, Signor Ludovico, did you get hold of all this foolery?"

(2).

La Garfagnana was a district in the Appenines, infested by robbers, of which Duke Alphonso, of Ferrara, made Ariosto Governor, as a means of relieving his necessitous condition.—ED.

(3).

The "Henriade" was printed in England, it would appear, Voltaire himself allowing that when he composed it, it was *sans savoir ce que c'était qu'un poème épique*. Moreover, as it was then said, *Les Français n'ont pas la tête épique*.—ED.

(4).

The "Telemaque" was said to be a satire on the French Court. "Like Emile, the Plebeian Telemachus of J. J. Rousseau, this work is exclusively social and political. It is at once the critic and theorist of society and governments. It was intended to furnish the programme of a future reign, in which the Duke of Burgundy was to be the Telemachus, and Fénélon the Mentor."—*Lamartine's European Celebrities (Translation)*.

CHAPTER XI.

(1).

"When I turn 30 I will turn devout. I feel a great vocation that way in Catholic Churches, and when I hear the organ."—Lord B. to Mr. Murray, April 2, 1817.

CHAPTER XII.

(1).

"I am taking a wife," said a friend to Rousseau. "What good qualities has she?" he replied. "She is handsome;" and the philosopher wrote down *Zero* (0)." She is rich;" and he inscribed another *Zero*. "And young;" a third (0). "And of noble birth;" again another (0). "And good tempered." And the philosopher placed a 1 before the four *Zeros*, to show that from this quality alone all the others received value.—ED.

(2).

Some of the opening stanzas of this poem are of great beauty and merit.

" Many a vanish'd year and day,
And battle's breath and tempest's rage,
Have passed o'er Corinth, yet she stands
A fortress formed to freedom's hands;
The keystone of a land that still,
Though fall'n, looks proudly from that hill."
. . . . . . &c.—*Siege of Corinth*.

(3).

" Around him some mysterious circle thrown,
Repell'd approach, and show'd him still alone;
With thought of years in phantom-chase misspent,
And wasteful powers for better purpose lent;
And fiery passions that had poured their wrath
In hurried desolation o'er his path."—*Lara*.

CHAPTER XIII.

(1).

" The day before yesterday I proposed to Lady Byron. I had no idea of doing so."—*Life by Bulwer.*—See also *Moore*.

" It had been predicted by Mrs. Williams that 27 was to be a dangerous age for me: The fortune-telling witch was right; it was destined to prove so. I shall never forget the 2nd of January! Lady Byron was the only unconcerned person present; Lady Noel, her mother, cried; I trembled like a leaf, made the wrong responses, and after the ceremony, called her Miss Millbank."—*Life by Bulwer.*—See also *Moore*.

(2).

Giovanni, D. G. J., the famous publicist, who died at Milan in 1835. His Life has been written by Cantù.

(3).

Manzoni, author of the best Italian Romance, the famous "I Promessi Sposi."

(4).

"S'opre d'arte e d 'ingegno, amore e zelo.
D'onore, han premio ovver perdono in terra,
Deh non sea, prego, il mio pregar deluso."

(5).

"His home was almost daily beset by duns; and his house, nine times during 1815, in possession of bailiffs," &c.—*Moore's Life*, (1830), vol. 1, p. 650.

(6)

As one of the Drury Lane Committee, and referring to Mrs. Martyn. —"To the falsehoods concerning his greenroom intimacies, and particularly with one beautiful actress with whom he had hardly even exchanged a single word, I have already adverted," &c.   . . . . , —*Moore's Life* (1830), vol. 1, p. 653.

(7).

See *Moore's Life.*—"You asked me if no cause was assigned for this sudden resolution (Lady Byron's resolve)—if I formed no conjecture about the cause? I will tell you. I have prejudices about women. I do not like to see them eat: Rousseau makes Julie *un peu gourmande*; but that is not at all according to my taste. I do not like to be interrupted when I am writing. Lady Byron did not attend to these whims of mine. The only harsh thing I ever remember saying to her was one evening shortly before our parting. I was standing before the fire, ruminating upon the embarrassment of my affairs, and other annoyances, when Lady Byron came up and said—"Byron, am I in your way?" to which I replied, "Damnably!" I was afterwards sorry, and reproached myself for the expression; but it escaped me unconsciously—involuntarily: I hardly knew what I said. I heard afterwards that Mrs. Charlemont had been the means of poisoning Lady Noel's mind against me. . . . . that she had employed herself and others in watching me in London . . . . . &c. There was one act of which I might justly have complained, and which was unworthy of anyone but such a *confidante*. I allude to the breaking open my writing desk . . . . ." &c.—*Conversations with T. Medwin, Esq.* (on which after-dinner confidences, some doubts have been expressed).

(8).

Thus, in a Quixotic romance, which remained unfinished and unpublished, where, under the mask of an Andalusian, he alluded to his own case. And in Don Juan, Canto 1:—

" And then, this best and meekest woman bore
    With such serenity her husband's woes,
Just as the Spartan ladies did of yore,
    Who saw their spouses killed, and nobly chose
Never to say a word about them more—
    Calmly she heard each calumny that rose;
    And saw his agonies with such sublimity,
    That all the world exclaimed ' What magnamimity !' " &c.

(9).

This poem is taken from the *Conversations of Lady Blessington with Lord Byron at Geneva*, and published in the *New Monthly Magazine*.

In the Mystery of Cain, when this first of homicides, accursed of all would flee to the desert, he says to his sister Adah :—

"Dost thou not fear to dwell with one who hath done this?
Adah: I fear no thing except to leave thee, much as I
  Shrink from the deed which leaves thee brotherless—
  I must not speak of this—it is between thee and
  The Great God!"

These verses were written immediately after the failure of the negotiation for reconciliation, and were not intended for publication.—Note to *Byron's Works*, Murray, 1850.

CHAPTER XV.

(1).

Amongst other discrepancies, so to speak, he himself says :—"He (Rousseau) could never ride nor swim, nor was 'cunning of fence.' I am an excellent swimmer, a decent though not at all a dashing rider, (having staved in a rib at 18, in the course of scampering), and was sufficient of fence, particularly of the Highland broadsword,—not u bad boxer, when I could keep my temper, which was difficult, but which I swore to do ever since I knocked down Mr. Purling, and put his kneepan out (with the gloves on), in Angelo and Jackson's sparring rooms in 1806, during the sparring. I was, besides, a very fair cricketer—one of the Harrow Eleven, when we played against Eton in 1805."—*Moore's Life* (1847)—"Detached Thoughts."

CHAPTER XVI.

(1).

"Simplon is magnificent in its nature and art—both God and man have done wonders—to say nothing of the devil," &c.—Letter to Murray, Milan, Oct. 15, 1816.

(2).

"The Italians I have encountered are very intelligent and agreeable. In a few days I am to meet Monti," &c.—*Ibid*, from *Moore's Life*, p. 44, vol. 2.

(3).

"The Benacus with its *fluctibus et fremitu*."—Letter to Moore, Verona, Nov. 6, 1816.

CHAPTER XVII.

(1).

"Did I tell you that I have translated from the Armenian two epistles between St. Paul and the Corinthians, not to be found in our version?"—Letter to Moore, Venice, March 31, 1817.

(2).

"The 'Helen' of Canova (in the possession of Madame Albrizzi), is, without exception, the most perfectly beautiful of human conceptions, &c."—Letter to Murray, Nov. 25, 1816.

(3).

" Of painting I know nothing; but like a Guercino—a picture of Abraham putting away Hagar and Ishmael—which seems to be natural and goodly."—Letter to Murray, Milan, Oct. 15, 1816.

Yet a perfectly competent judge, Mons. Beyle (de Stendhahl), in a letter to Mdlle. L. S. Belloc, relates:—"Signor di B. induced me to accompany Lord Byron to the Brera Gallery; I witnessed with admiration the depth of feeling with which this great poet mastered the beauties of painters the most opposite in style: Raphael, Guercino, Zuini, Titian, &c. The 'Hagar put away by Abraham' of Guercino electrified him; from that moment admiration rendered us silent; he improvised for the space of one hour, and better, I think, than Madame de Stüel."—*Œuvres Posthumes de Stendhahl* (V. Appendix), Paris, 1824.

(4).

Moore's Life, 1830, p. 104, vol. II.

(5).

For the 4th Canto of Childe Harold, Lord Byron received £2,000; but it can hardly be deemed an excess of generosity on the part of the publisher, Murray.

(6).

"Marianna, then in her 22nd year, is, in her appearance, altogether like an antelope. She has the large, black, oriental eyes, with that peculiar expression in them, &c."—Letter to Moore, Venice, Nov. 11, 1816.

CHAPTER XVIII.

(1).

"Byron's dinner, when the Fornarina was his companion, consisted, he was assured, of but four *beccafichi*, of which the Fornarina ate three, leaving him hungry."—*Moore's Life*, vol. 2, p. 208.

CHAPTER XIX.

(1).

"There is still in the Doge's Palace the Black Veil painted over Faliero's picture, &c."—Letter to Murray, April 2, 1817.

(2).

Dr. Faustus, the "Don Juan," it may be said of the north, lived, it appears, in the beginning of the 16th century. His adventures were related in an old German book, translated into many languages, and from which Marlow (Shakespeare's contemporary), derived his play, "The Tragic History of Dr. Faust." Lessing also intended to compose two tragedies from it, but they did not see the light. Klingerne, however, worked out or upon it a philosophic romance, "The life and actions of Faust, and his visit to the Infernal Regions." One would rather say that from Goethe's "Faust" was taken Byron's "Deformed Transformed."

(3).

" Goethe's 'Faust' I never read, for I don't know German; but Mr. Lewis, in 1816, translated most of it to me, and I was naturally much struck by it; but it was the Steinbach and the Jungfrau and something else, more than Faustus, that made me write Manfred. The first scene, however, and that of Faustus are very similar."—Letter to Murray, *Moore's Life*, vol. 2, p. 230.—Again, Byron says —"I wrote a sort of mad drama, for the sake of introducing the Alpine scenery, &c."—Letter to Murray, Venice, March 25, 1817.

(4).

The opening lines certainly bear out this panegyric:—
" It is the hour, when from the boughs,
The nightingale's high note is heard,
It is the hour, when lovers' vows
Seem sweet in every whisper'd word,
And gentle winds and waters near
Make music to the lonely ear," &c.

CHAPTER XXI.

(1).

The great object which Diderot and the Encyclopædists had in view,
according to the biographical judgment of the day, was to sap the
foundation of all religion.

(2).

"Now, my sere fancy falls into the yellow leaf,
And imagination droops his pinion,
And the sad truth, which hovers o'er my desk,
Turns what was once romantic to burlesque."
Don Juan, Canto 4.

Only 50 copies of this poem were first intended to be printed for private
circulation.—ED.

(3).

In Greece, he'd sing some sort of hymn like this t'ye:
" The Isles of Greece, the Isles of Greece!
Where burning Sappho loved and sung
Where grew the Arts of War and peace—!
Whence Delos rose, and Phœbus sprung," &c., &c.

(4).

The maid of Saragoza used to walk on the Prado during Byron's tour
in Spain, by order of the Junta, adorned with medals and orders.—ED.

(5).

" * * * * The 5th Canto is so far from being the last of Don Juan, that
it is hardly the beginning. I meant to take him the tour of Europe, with
a proper mixture of siege, battle, and adventure, and to make him
finish as Anacharsis Cloots in the French Revolution." — Letter to
Murray, July, 6, 1821.—*Moore's Life*, vol. 2, 498, 1830.

(6).

Again: "Poor Juan shall be guillotined in the French Revolution!
What do you think of my plot? It shall have 24 books, too, the
legitimate number."—*Conversations with Medwin*.

(7).

"The truth is that in these days the grand *primum mobile* of England is
cant; cant political, cant poetical, cant religious, cant moral; but always
cant, multiplied through all the varieties of life."—Letter to Mr. Murray
from Ravenna.

(8).

" In the preface to Cantos 6, 7, 8, Byron gives, amongst much that is
argumentative, if not convincing, two quotations from Voltaire:
" La pudeur s'est enfuite des cœurs, et s'est refugiée sur les lèvres; . . . .
Plus les mœurs sont dépravées, plus les expressions deviennent mesurées.
. . . on croit regagner en langage ce qu'on a perdu en vertu."

CHAPTER XXII.

(1).

The works of Alexander Pope, Esq., in verse and prose, containing the
principal notes of Drs. Warburton and Warton, &c. &c.

(2).

The anathema and the ball room scene are probably both masterpieces in their way, and scarcely to be rivalled in any language.—Ed.

(3).

"*Barbarigo.* Is it true that you have written in your books of commerce—the wealthy practice of your highest nobles—'Doge Foscari, my debtor for the death of Marco and Pietro Loredano, my sire and uncle?'
"*Loredano*: It is written thus.
"*Barbarigo*: And will you leave it uncrased?
"*Loredano*: Till balanced."   —*The Two Foscari*, Act 1.

(4).

"Oh! thou would'st doubtless have me set up edicts,—
'Obey the King—contribute to his treasure—
Recruit his phalanx—spill your blood at bidding,
Fall down and worship, or get up and toil.'
Or this—'Sardanapalus on this spot.
Slew fifty thousand of his enemies.
These are their sepulchres, and this his trophy.'"
                      —*Sardanapalus*, Act 1. Scene 2.

(5).

"Listen, the Church was throng'd
     The hymn was raised
          Te Deum pealed from Nations,
               Rather than from Choirs, in one great cry
          Of God be praised
               For one day's peace after thrice ten years
          Each bloodier than the former, &c."

CHAPTER XXIII.

(1).

Adopting the opinion of Cuvier that the world had been destroyed many times before the creation of Adam.

(2.)

"If 'Cain' be blasphemous, 'Paradise Lost' is blasphemous; and the very words of the Oxford gentleman 'Evil, be thou my good', are from that poem, from the mouth of Satan, and is there anything more in that of Lucifer in the Mystery? 'Cain' is nothing more than a drama, not a piece of argument. If Lucifer and Cain speak as the first murderer or the first rebel may be supposed to speak, surely all the rest of the personages talk also according to their characters—and the stronger passions have ever been permitted to the drama, &c. I have even avoided introducing the Deity as in Scripture (though Milton does and not very wisely,) but have adopted his Angel as sent to Cain instead, on purpose to avoid shocking any feelings, &c."—*Letter to Murray*, who had been threatened with a prosecution on account of this publication.—*Conversations with Medwin*, note, pp. 192—3.

(3)

"Bring forth the horse!—the horse was brought.
     In truth he was a noble stéed
     A Tartar of the Ukraine breed
Who look'd as though the speed of thought
     Were in his limbs, but he was wild
Wild as the wild deer and untaught!
     With bit and bridle undefiled."
· Or:—"But let me on. Theresa's form,
     Methinks it glides before me now,
     Between me and yon chestnut's bough,
     The memory is so quick and warm—

And yet I find no words to tell
The shape of her I loved so well."
"She had the Asiatic eye.
Such as our Turkish neighbourhood
Hath mingled with our Turkish blood."   . &c., &c.

(4).

" And I was looked upon somewhat as the great Napoleon of the realms
of rhyme:—but Juan was my Moscow, and Faliero my Leipsic, and my
Mont St. Jean* seems Cain.—*Don Juan*, Canto II.
And in a letter, " Poor Napoleon! Little could he have divined to
what a turn of the wheel might reduce him."

*The French name for Waterloo.

(5).

" I have promised to contribute, and shall probably make it a vehicle
for some occasional poems; for instance, I mean to translate Ariosto
(*Medwin*, p 403). I was strongly advised by Tom Moore, long ago, not
to have any connection with such a company as Hunt, and Shelley, and
Co.: but I have pledged myself, and, besides, could not now, if I had
ever so great a disinclination for the scheme, disappoint all Hunt's hopes.
He has a large family, has undertaken a long journey (to Pisa), and
undergone a long series of persecutions."—"Hunt, when party feeling ran
high against Byron, was the only editor of a paper, the only literary man,
who dared say a word in his justification."—*Medwin*, pp. 402-3.

CHAPTER XXIV.

(1).

At the particular request of the Countess Guiccioli, he wrote, "I have
promised not to continue Don Juan, &c."—Letter to Murray, Pisa,
July 6, 1821.
"Lord Byron told me that La Contessa Guiccioli had repeatedly
asked him to discontinue Don Juan, as its immorality shocked her,"
&c.   "To please her," said Byron, "I gave it up for some time,
and have only got permission to continue it on condition of making my
hero a more moral person. I shall end by making him turn Methodist;
this will please the English and be an *amende honorable* for his sins and
mine."—*Conversations with Lady Blessington.*—p. 206.
Again: Letter to Murray, Ravenna, Sept. 4, p. 134:—" You say nothing
of the note* I enclosed to you, which will explain why I agreed to
discontinue Don Juan, (at Madame G's request), but you are so grand
and sublime, and occupied, that one would think, instead of publishing
for the Board of Longitude, that you were trying to discover it."

* In this note, so highly honourable to the fair writer, she says " Remember,
my Byron, the promise you have made me . . . . Never shall I be able to
tell you the satisfaction which I feel for your sacrifice." . . . . She adds, in a
note : " Mi rincresce solo che Don Giovani non resta all Inferno."

CHAPTER XXV.

(1.)

Letter to Murray, Venice, Oct. 29. 1819.—" I gave to Moore, who is
gone to Rome, my Life, in MS. in 78 folio sheets, brought down to 1816.
But this I put into his hands for his care, as he has some other MSS.
of mine—a journal kept in 1814, &c. Neither are for publication during
my life, but when I am cold, you may do what you please. In the
meantime, if you like to read them, you may show them to anybody
you like—I care not. The life is Memoranda and not confessions.
I have left out all my *loves* (except in a general way), and many
other of the most important things, &c.

"Finally, I gave them to Moore, or rather to Moore's little boy at Venice. I remember saying 'There are £2,000 for you, my young friend.' I made one reservation in the gift—that they were not to be published till after my death."—*Medwin's Conversations with Lord Byron.* —p. 40.

(2).

Alfieri bought in England, it is said, not less than 14 horses.

(3).

The Burning of the Temple of Diana of Ephesus, 356 B.C.

CHAPTER XXVIII.

(1).

"To my mind, in fact, praise it who will, the conception introduced in the last Pilgrimage of Childe Harold, as versified by Lamartine, appears unchristian. The poet, at the point of death, is summoned by the Angel of Judgment to choose between two urns, the one of life (mortal), the other of death (fatal), and with no other lights save those of reason, genius, and faith. But the torch of faith he rejects; that of reason is extinguished by the wings of the night birds; while that of genius is put out in the attempt to revive it. In the obscurity, then, he chooses the urn of evil, and is lost. Oh! the religion of love, of our Christ that wished not the death of a sinner, and

> 'Dalle stanche ceneri
> Spende ogni ria parola.' "

CHAPTER XXXI.

(1).

Perhaps the lines on Lara bear out this view :—

> "Left by his sire, too young such loss to know,
> Lord of himself,—that heritage of woe,
> That fearful empire which the human breast,
> But holds to rob the heart within of rest!
> With none to check, and few to point, in time,
> The thousand paths that slope the way to crime;
> Then, when he most required commandment, then
> Had Lara's daring boyhood govern'd men."
> . . . . &c., &c.

(2)

> "When some proud son of man returns to earth,
> Unknown to glory, but upheld by birth,
> The sculptor's art exhausts the pomp of woe,
> And storied urns record who rest below;
> When all is done, upon the tomb is seen,
> Not what he was, but what he should have been;
> But the poor dog, in life the firmest friend,
> The first to welcome, foremost to defend,
> Whose honest heart is still his master's own,
> Who labours, fights, lives, breathes for him alone,
> Unhonor'd falls, unnoticed all his worth,
> Denied in heaven the soul he held on earth.

> . . . .
> Ye! who perchance behold this simple urn,
> Pass on—it honours none you wish to mourn:
> To mark a friend's remains, these stones arise;
> I never knew but one, and here he lies."
> —*Inscription on the monument of "Boatswain," a New-foundland dog.*

APPENDIX.

No 1. Preface.

The *Dizionario Biografico* of Cafardi, 1879, assigns Brivio, Castello Milanese, as the birth-place of Cantù, in December, 1807. It mentions also that he is Chevalier and Chancellor of the Italian order of Civil Merit. From the Imperial Dictionary of Biography we gather that he has been decorated by many European sovereigns, and that his name is enrolled in most Academies and Societies in Europe.

No. 2. Chap. 13, p. 22.

On Lord Byron's conjugal infelicity, and the public scandal, so to speak, resulting therefrom, Macaulay has written :—(Essay—*Moore's Life of Byron.*) " We know no spectacle so ridiculous as the British public in one of its periodical fits of morality, &c. . . . . . . But we are not aware that there is before the world, substantiated by credible or even tangible evidence, a single fact indicating that Lord Byron was more to blame than any other man who is on bad terms with his wife, &c." . . The great essayist finally adds : . . . . "It is certain that the interest which Byron excited during his life is without a parallel in literary history."

No. 3. Chap. 21, p. 42.

For a minute disquisition, and observations on the characteristics of Lord Byron's disposition and temperament, during at least his sojourn in Italy, the enquiring reader is referred to the works of Henry Beyle (De Steudhahl), his letters to Louise S. du Belloc and his friends, and *L'Histoire de la Peinture*.

No. 4. Chap. 22, p 46.

Marino Faliero. Lord Byron acknowledges to have slightly altered the tragic history of this Dege, though he had studied the subject for four years, and had consulted thereon Sanuto, Vettor, Daru, Sismondi, and others. A brief account of the melancholy story of Faliero, taken, it would seem, from the *Chronicles of Giustiniani*, may be read in the *Lives of the Doges* by Eric M'Kay, published in Venice in 1878.

No. 5. Chap. 24, p. 53.

La Contessa Guiccioli, afterwards married to the Marquis de Boissy, is the author of the work *Lord Byron jugé par les témoins de sa Vie*, published in Paris in 1868.

No. 6. Chap. 26, p. 62.

Alfieri, of historical note as the second husband of the widow of Prince Charles Edward Stuart, styled the " Young Pretender," and besides his linguistic attainments and notoriety as a man of gallantry, was of high repute as a dramatist. He enjoyed the singular reputation of having written a tragedy—*Cleopatra*, and a burlesque thereon, both alike successful.

No. 7. Chap. 31, p. 73.

Lamartine :—" Le dernier chant de Childe Harold :—

. . . . . .

" Ecoute ! et recommence !
Mais tremble ! car tu vas tirer ton dernier sort !

"Au lieu le plus obscur, où, sur ces champs de mort,
La nuit semble epaissir les ombres taciturnes ;
L'ange du jugement vient de placer deux urnes,
Dont l' uniforme aspect trompe l'œil et la main."

No. 8.

LINES ON THE DEATH OF LORD BYRON.

Byron! with feelings deep I trace these views :
Here, o'er this awful mountain scene, so rude,
Oft thy young eagle fancy loved to muse,
Rapt in the sad stern joys of solitude.

Here, lonely wandering 'mid these barren rocks,
Thy mighty soul imbibed celestial fire—
Here, in this wild abode of foldless flocks,
Did early genius thy proud heart inspire,—
Here would'st thou linger on this frowning peak,
Gazing with rapture at the fearful storm—
All fearless thou—thy godlike mind would seek
To give the lightning's flash embodied form.

And thou art gone! Thy earthly race is run
And thou art gone!—too soon for hapless Greece—
Too soon for liberty—has set thy glorious sun!
That trampled land! when shall her bondage cease ?
To thee, like Homer, time's stern self shall bow,
Thy fame, thy cherished name. shall deathless be,
When Britain has become, what Troy is now,
A blank, a doubt, on vast Eternity.

F. C.

Lord Byron passed some portion of his boyhood in the vicinity of Loch-na-Garr mountain, and frequently remained on that mountain, and the neighbouring hills, whole days alone.

Isle of Skye, November, 1825.

See also the poem, "Lachin-y-Gair."—ED.

No. 9.

HONOURS IN WESTERN GREECE—PAID TO BYRON AT HIS DEATH.
Provisional Government of Greece.
Art. 1185.

18. 4. 1824.

Until, therefore, the final determination of the National Government be known, and by virtue of the powers with which it has been pleased to invest me, I hereby decree:—

1st.—To-morrow morning, at daylight, thirty-seven minute guns will be fired from the Grand Battery, being the number which corresponds with the age of the illustrious deceased.

2nd.—All the public offices, even the Tribunals, are to remain closed for three successive days.

3rd.—All the shops, except those in which provisions or medicines are sold, will also be shut; and it is strictly enjoined that every species of public amusement, and other demonstrations of festivity at Easter, shall be suspended.

4th.—A general mourning will be observed for twenty-one days.

5th.—Prayers and general service are to be offered up in all the churches.

(Signed)   A. MAVROCORDATO.

Given at Missolonghi,
18th April, 1824.

The Editor of the little work now offered for perusal has endeavoured, in almost all cases, to verify the statements of the Italian legislator, historian, and author; but he cannot consider himself responsible for statements or opinions enunciated by Signor Cantù, and which lack the authority of Lord Byron's biographers or correspondents.

Finally, the Editor of Signor Cantù's instructive Essay has not deemed it necessary to advert to the historic doubts on the Life of Homer, as portrayed in Chapter X.; nor to the somewhat obscure reference to the Mysteries of Isis on a page following: he has preferred to leave such paragraphs, as are left some passages of Scripture, to the belief or understanding or learning of the reader.

A. K.

Mr. Redway's Publications

Printed on large hand-made paper, with India Proof Illustrations mounted as Frontispiece and Tailpiece.   Price 10s. 6d.

The Worship of Priapus.

Being an account of the Fête of St. Cosmo and Damiano, celebrated at Isernia. In a letter to Sir Joseph Banks, President of the Royal Society. By Sir William Hamilton, Minister at the Court of Naples. To which is added Some Account of Phallic Worship, principally derived from the Work of Richard Payne Knight. Edited, with Preface and Notes, by Hargrave Jennings, author of "The Rosicrucians."

₊ *Only* 100 *copies printed, each numbered. After* 75 *copies have been subscribed for, the price will be raised to One Guinea.*

In demy 8vo, elegantly printed on Dutch hand-made paper, and bound in parchment-paper cover.   Price 1s,

The Scope and Charm of Antiquarian Study.

By John Batty, F.R.Hist.S., Member of the Yorkshire Archæological and Topographical Association,

"Mr. Batty, who is one of those folks Mr. Dobson styles ' gleaners after time,' has clearly and concisely summed up, in the space of a few pages, all the various objects which may legitimately be considered to come within the scope of antiquarian study."—*Academy.*

THACKERAY AND CRUIKSHANK.

An Essay on the Genius of George Cruikshank.

By " Theta " (William Makepeace Thackeray), reprinted with Illustrations from the *Westminster Review*, with a new Portrait of Cruikshank engraved on Wood, and a Prefatory Essay on Thackeray as an Art Critic, by W. E. Church, Secretary of the Urban Club. *In preparation.*

Some Passages in the Early Life of Charles Dickens.

By Hargrave Jennings, Author of " The Rosicrucians," &c.
In preparation.

Tobacco Talk and Smokers' Gossip.

An Amusing Miscellany of Fact and Anecdote relating to " The Great Plant " in all its Forms and Uses, including a Selection from Nicotian Literature; the whole interspersed with Woodcuts and Engravings. Compiled and arranged by Ernest E. Darke. Edited by George Redway. *In preparation.*